Thank you!

MR. DARCY'S KISS

KRISTA LAKES

Krista Lakes

ZIRCONIA PUBLISHING, INC.

ABOUT THIS BOOK

Rich.
British.
Hot as hell.

ELIZABETH BENNETT HAS NEVER APPRECIATED any of these traits in a man. So when Mr. Darcy, billionaire British playboy and GQ's Bachelor of the Year, meets her at a function, she's surprised at how attracted she is to him.

That is until he puts his foot in his big, arrogant mouth.

The slap that she gave him got her thrown out of the biggest fundraiser of the year, but the mark she left on Mr. Darcy won't leave his mind.

The second time that they meet "on accident", he turns up the arrogance even more.

The third time, he tries flowers.

By the fourth time, he's wearing a cup to protect himself.

Mr. Darcy is the last man in the world that Elizabeth could ever be with. However, love makes fools of us all, and the one man that she can't stand is the one man she can't resist.

Can Mr. Darcy's kiss win over the heart of Elizabeth Bennett?

Join New York Times bestselling author Krista Lakes in this modern retelling of Jane Austen's beloved *"Pride and Prejudice"*.

I KEPT DANCING across the dance floor, moving my hips and having fun. I could see Lydia out of the corner of my eye shaking her booty and having a great time. For once, I wasn't worried about her getting kicked out. She seemed to be behaving herself.

A cute man came up and started dancing with me. He was mid-height with blonde hair and a couple of tattoos peeking out from under his shirtsleeves. I offered my hand, and he spun me into him, putting his hands on my hips and moving with me to the music.

At first, the dance was fun. Cute-guy kept his hands on my hips, pulling me into his body and moving to the music. It was worlds away better than dancing with Collins, but then he started going too far. He grabbed my ass instead of my hips, and he didn't let me go as he thrust his pelvis into me.

I stepped away, no longer enjoying what was going on. I wanted to dance, not to be groped.

"Come on, baby," he said over the music, flashing me what I assumed was his best smile. He was no longer Cute-guy. He was now Cute-but-awful guy. "It's just for fun."

"I think I'm done," I said, turning to leave, but he grabbed my hand.

"Just another dance, baby," he cooed. "I'll behave. Until you don't want me to."

I tried to wrench my arm from his grasp, but he was much bigger and stronger than me. I wasn't sure what to do. Should I play nice until he let me go and then run? Should I kick him in the balls? Scream bloody murder?

"She said she's done," a strong voice said behind me. I turned to find Mr. Darcy out on the dance floor. For the first time since meeting him, I was glad to see him.

"Wait your turn," Cute-but-awful guy told him. He still had my wrist in his hand.

"No," Mr. Darcy said, putting his hand on my shoulder. He looked dangerous. "Either you leave now, or they help you out."

He nodded to the three muscle-bound bouncers in black watching them. Cute-but-awful guy dropped my wrist.

"You need to chill, man," Cute-but-awful guy said. He blew me a kiss and walked away.

I stood there on the dance floor breathing hard even though I wasn't moving. Mr. Darcy had rescued me. I knew I could have done it myself, but his method was way more effective and didn't involve bodily harm.

"Thank you," I told him over the music.

He shrugged like it was nothing. "May I have the next dance?"

He held out his hand, waiting for me to take it.

I hesitated. Not because I thought he would end up like Cute-but-awful guy, or because I didn't want to. I really *wanted* to dance with Mr. Darcy. I wanted to dance and then do so much more than dancing. And that's what scared me.

"You may," I replied.

∾

"Because I want to know why," I replied, taking a step toward him. I wanted to get under his skin and annoy him as much as he annoyed me. I wanted him to think of me the way I did him: often and without meaning to.

"I'll tell you anything you want to know," he said, his voice low and dangerous. He was close to me now. I didn't remember taking quite this many steps into him, but I was close enough now to smell his cologne. I could see the blues and grays of his eyes and the small spot he missed shaving near his earlobe.

How did he infuriate me so easily? Why did being near him cause my heart to go crazy and my ability to think disappear? I glared up at him, riled and looking for a fight. I wanted to get a reaction out of him. I wanted him to react to me.

I wanted to knock him down and kiss him, and I wasn't sure it was in that order. The space at the arch of my legs ached for something only he could give me. I hated him, yet my body wanted his touch. Lust surged through me in hot waves.

I hated that I wanted him, but that only made me want him more.

How did he get under my skin and turn me on?

Without thinking, without my brain's permission, my body leaned forward and kissed him.

And oh, God, did it feel good.

Every part of my body sang with need and kissing him made it better and worse at the same time. He threaded his hand behind my head and into my hair, kissing me back.

And the man could kiss. His lips were soft, yet demanding. He tasted better than he had in any of my dreams. Sweet, yet rich with hints of champagne.

Before I knew what I was doing, I wrapped my arms

around his neck, not letting him go. I needed his kisses, his touch, and so much more. I needed him more than I needed to breathe. I hated him and needed him in equal parts.

What in the world had he done to me? I went from hating him to wanting to screw him in the space of a single kiss.

"We should go someplace less public." He broke the kiss just long enough to whisper the words, and even then that was too long.

I nodded, hating that he pulled away from me. My body ached to feel him against me, and even though I knew I would get more, I hated that I didn't have him that instant.

He grabbed my hand. With my lips still tingling from Mr. Darcy's kiss, he pulled me away from the crowd.

To my writer friends
Thanks for keeping me sane (ish)

Chapter 1

"Will you hurry up? We're going to be late," Lydia complained. She leaned against the bathroom door and watched as I finished putting the last touches on my mascara.

"And what?" I asked, turning to look at her. "We'll miss the waiters walking around with the little trays of fancy hot dogs you don't like? You'll live. Promise."

My little sister rolled her eyes at me. For being twenty-one, she still had all the abilities of a teenager in the eye-roll department. She took a deep breath like I was trying all of her patience and checked her hair in the mirror one more time.

"I guess it *is* fashionable to be late," she said, smoothing down her dark hair. "We'll look more important and more people will be able to see us arrive."

I couldn't help but shake my head. It was hard to believe we were related sometimes. We both had the same slim build, dark hair and dark eyes, but the similarities ended there. She was impulsive, naive, and fame-hungry, which drove me absolutely batty. She was sure she was the center of the universe.

I, at least, acknowledged that I was only the center of the solar system, not the entire universe.

"Have either of you seen my silver earrings?" our room-mate Jane asked, poking her head into the bathroom and looking around. "Oh, you're wearing them, Lydia."

"They look so much better on me," Lydia replied with a shrug. "You should wear the blue ones. They bring out your eyes."

"Can you at least ask next time?" Jane asked, crossing her arms. She managed to look beautiful and statuesque even though she was angry. She always managed to look beautiful and statuesque.

"Fine," Lydia replied with another classic eye roll. "But you know I'm right."

It was Jane's turn to roll her eyes.

"Lizzie, you're sure this is a fancy, exclusive event, right?" Lydia asked, pushing up her cleavage in her skintight black dress. "Famous people will be there?"

I sighed. "Yes, Lydia. It's the main fund-raising event for the two major hospitals in New York City. It's super fancy, and it's super lucky I even won these tickets. We couldn't afford to go otherwise."

"Good," she replied. She frowned as she watched me put my mascara away. "Elizabeth Bennet, you need to put more mascara on. I can barely see your eyes."

"Are you serious?" I asked her. I was already wearing about ten pounds of makeup. I felt like I'd been getting ready and putting makeup on all day.

"Yes," Lydia replied, reaching into my makeup bag and handing me back my mascara. "You need to look like you belong at this party."

"Why can't I just be me?" I asked her, not putting any more mascara on yet.

"Because you aren't fancy," Lydia replied. "You're smart, and you're sweet, but I swear, you'd go in a ponytail and your work scrubs if I let you."

"No, I'd at least wear this dress. I like the fancy dress," I informed her. The floor-length gown hugged my curves as it made its silky dark blue way to my feet. It had just enough of a hint of sparkle in the fabric to make me feel like it had been blessed by a fairy godmother. The dress was awesome. I stuck my tongue out at Lydia, and she just pushed the mascara at me again.

"I'm glad you'd at least wear the dress," Lydia replied. "It is designer. I still can't believe you found a Prada dress. You look amazing, but you have to finish it. More mascara."

I sighed, but I put on another layer. I looked up in the mirror and shook my head at the stunning woman looking back at me. Lydia was right. I looked amazing, but I didn't look like me. I looked like a Barbie-doll version of me. I couldn't imagine how women did this every day. It was exhausting getting this done up.

"Oh, did you two hear?" Lydia asked watching me like a hawk. She motioned for another swipe of mascara. "The penthouse of our building is rented out for the rest of the year."

"Really? I thought it was considered too expensive for the market." Jane looked surprised as she put in the blue earrings. They really did complement her cornflower blue eyes perfectly. They even brought out the soft gold in her hair. Not that we'd ever tell Lydia she was right.

"It is *way* overpriced," Lydia confirmed. "But, supposedly, it's this business guy worth millions. The money means nothing to him. He just wants to be near Central Park while he opens some new business ventures, so he's renting the place. It's so exciting."

I stepped back from the mirror. "Why are you so excited? He's not an actor. I thought you wanted to be a movie star."

"I *will* be a movie star," Lydia corrected me. "But he's rich. Rich buys access to fame. Famous people hang out with rich people."

"I still don't get it," I told her, shaking my head. "How is meeting this guy going to make you an actress?"

"If I can be arm candy for a night, or if he meets me in the elevator with his famous friends- I'm in," she explained. "I'd be famous in a heartbeat. Once I'm famous, I'll have all the roles I can handle. It's an opportunity most people would give their right arm for."

"Oh, I get it." I nodded and put the mascara away. "New neighbor is definitely arm-chopping off potential."

I motioned to my face, and Lydia nodded her approval before leaving the bathroom. I turned to Jane when she was gone. "I'm surprised we don't see more arm-less people walking around given the kinds of opportunities here."

Jane snorted and pushed me out of the bathroom.

Lydia was waiting impatiently by the front door of our apartment with our jackets. They looked shabby compared to our gowns, but there was nothing to do about it now. Lydia had found a company that rented high-end clothing, so we all dressed to the nines in clothes we could never afford. Other than our jackets, of course.

The three of us were going to the most significant hospital fund-raising gala in New York City. Every year, the two major hospitals joined forces to put on a black tie event. It was next to impossible to get tickets, but since I worked at one of the hospitals, I had managed to win some at a work raffle. Lydia was sure that someone rich and famous would notice her, and thus this gala was her ticket to fame and fortune.

"Are you two finally ready?" We nodded, and she closed her eyes and took a deep breath. "You've got this, Lydia. It's your night to be a star." She peeked one eye open and glared at Jane and I. "Don't screw this up for me."

It was my turn to roll my eyes. I wasn't as good at it as Lydia, but I could roll with the best of them. Lydia ignored me and walked out into the hallway. I followed, doing my best not to trip on my dress.

"Hurry up," she called as she pressed the button for the elevator. "Unless the new penthouse guy is in the elevator. Then you two can be as slow as you like so I can talk to him."

Jane closed the apartment door behind us. "You and your dreams," she said, shaking her head and smiling. "I hope they all come true."

It wasn't crazy to think that a millionaire might be living in our building soon. Jane's parents had purchased the apartment back in the eighties as an investment property. It was just a hop and a skip away from Central Park, and what had once been considered a sketchy neighborhood was now prime real estate. The apartment was worth well over ten times what they paid for it.

Jane owned the apartment now. She shared it with Lydia and me for practically nothing since we were as good as sisters. Jane's parents died a few years ago, and we were the closest thing she had left to family. It was the three of us against all of New York, and we had a fantastic apartment to work out of.

～

IT WAS a short cab ride to the Ritz Carlton hotel for the fundraiser. Since it was black tie only and incredibly exclusive, all of New York wanted to come. The place was packed with expensive cars and flashing camera lights. We stepped out onto the red carpet leading up to the main entrance and felt like movies stars.

I could see why Lydia wanted this feeling all the time.

Inside, beautiful people wearing beautiful clothing walked around the hotel. We dropped our coats off at the coat check, and for the rest of the night, there would be no way to tell that we didn't belong with the rich and famous.

I smoothed the silk fabric on my dark blue gown, glad I had listened to Lydia's advice on renting the dress. My go-to little black dress would not have fit in with all the designer gowns walking around. I would have felt incredibly out of place.

"Oh my god, oh my god, oh my god!" Lydia bounced up and down and pointed. "It's Layla Falls! She's here!"

"Who?" Jane asked, looking around. "Who fell?"

"No, Layla Falls, the movie star," Lydia explained, pointing Jane in the right direction. "She just released a new movie. She's so famous."

Lydia looked like she might faint with joy.

"I doubt you'll get close to her," I told her, pointing to the three men in dark suits wearing earpieces that stood beside the movie star.

"Oh, I will," Lydia assured me. "We're going to be best friends by the end of the night."

"You say she's famous?" Jane asked. "I don't recognize her."

"You don't recognize anyone if they aren't a French Post-Impressionist painter," Lydia replied to our friend. "She was in that action movie this summer. She's rumored to be making a medical drama next, so being here is probably research. Hospitals and all."

"Oh, I think I remember her now," Jane replied. She watched the actress for a moment and then shook her head, obviously still not recognizing her. "I'll go find us a table."

"Lizzie, can you teach me some medical words?" Lydia asked, watching her hero smile for the cameras across the room. "Maybe I can be an adviser to the film or something."

"I need a drink," I said, looking around the lobby for an escape from my sister. There was supposed to be an open bar, and if I was going to deal with my sister going after Layla all night, I was going to need some alcohol.

Lydia didn't even notice I had gone as I made my way to the bar. She just stared at her movie star dream with big eyes and hopeful sighs.

The bar was easy enough to find. It was where everyone was congregating. I looked around, taking in the sights. Everyone looked polished and rich. Lydia was right about me needing more mascara to fit in here. It felt like a very different world than the one of scrubs and stethoscopes I was comfortable with.

Jane waved to me from across the lobby as she and Lydia found a table. They were the only familiar faces in the crowd. I worked as a Cardiac ICU nurse, and the only reason I would ever interact with the people at this party was if they had a heart attack. I wasn't quite sure I would ever fit in with this level of wealth, or given the amount of makeup I was forced to wear to be here if I even wanted to.

"Two martinis and one long island ice tea, please," I informed the bartender once it was my turn. He quickly went to making my drinks as I waited patiently by the bar. I stood there, minding my own space when someone bumped directly into me, nearly knocking me over.

He was tall, dark, and handsome with eyes the color of the sea after a storm. I could have fallen in love with him right there, except for the dirty look he was shooting me. He glared at me like it was my fault for being in his way when he wasn't looking where he was going.

It was typical entitled rich guy. He thought he owned the world. There was no way I was apologizing for his mistake, though, so I just smiled sweetly up at him. "Can I help you?"

He made an annoyed sound and continued on his way. It was a shame he was a jerk. The man was good looking, and if he was at this party, probably rich. Unfortunately, he was obviously way too full of himself to apologize. He walked away with more swagger than any man deserved. Especially after being the bumper, not the bumpee.

My drinks arrived, and I managed to carry all three of them over the table without spilling. Lydia took a big sip while Jane thanked me.

"What should we do next?" I asked, taking a sip of my drink. It was nice and strong. I was going to have a great night.

"Let's go look at the silent auction," Jane suggested. "We can bid on the items while they're still in our price range and feel like we're helping to raise funds for the hospitals."

I chuckled. The silent auction was going to be full of things we could never hope to afford, but it still sounded like fun to go and see what they had.

"You two can do that," Lydia said, picking up her already half-empty drink and looking around the room. "I'm going to go mingle. I need to make friends with Layla."

"Good luck," I replied as she fluffed her hair. She put her chin up and walked away with a mission.

"Do you think she'll find someone to make her famous?" Jane asked.

"She'll probably have as much luck at it as we will winning something from the auction," I replied with a shake of my head. I wasn't betting on either.

Chapter 2

"*L*izzie, it's a Gustave Loiseau," Jane gasped, her hand to her mouth as she stared in wonder at lot number 327 of the auction. A lovely seascape hung on the wall. I could almost smell the warm sea air coming from the white sandy cliffs.

"It's very nice," I told her. I had no idea who the artist was, but whoever he was impressed Jane. Art was her thing, not mine, but I could see the love in her eyes for the small painting. It was more than just something lovely to look at for her. It was an expression of life itself.

"Are you sure I can't borrow twenty thousand dollars?" Jane asked, not taking her eyes from the painting. "This would look amazing in our living room."

"I have twenty dollars, and I'll buy you a print," I told her with a gentle smile. "Because you are right. It would look amazing in the living room."

Jane sighed and kept staring at the painting. Paintings, specifically old French ones, were her passion. When she wasn't working at her painting restoration job at the museum, she volunteered at the New York Met and taught art classes to children on the side. I wished I had the funds to purchase something like this for her. She would be one of the few people in the world to *really* appreciate it.

"There's a Monet over there," I told her, pointing to the next auction lot.

"Oh, I need to be rich," she murmured, her eyes lighting up as she moved to the next painting. "It's so perfect."

I chuckled and followed behind her as she joined a man inspecting the small painting. I paused to check the price tag on the Loiseau just in case. It was so far out of my price range that just looking at it hurt. The only way I would ever get Jane nice art was at the art museum gift shop.

"Look at the way he captures the light and the movement of the water," Jane said to the man, thinking he was me. Her hand moved through the air to demonstrate.

"The individual brush strokes are so beautiful," the man replied, motioning to the painting. He looked to be about the same age as Jane. "Precise, and yet imperfect."

Jane's eyes lit up as she turned to the man. "Yes! That's what makes a Monet a Monet. He was the first to use this style."

The man grinned at her, thrilled at finding a kindred soul. "What do you think about his use of color in his later paintings?"

That's when I carefully turned away. If he was going to ask Jane about one of her favorite topics, there was no way I was going to interrupt them. I knew very little about art compared to Jane, so I knew I wouldn't be able to contribute to the conversation anyway.

I wandered the auction a bit longer. There were some things that I was actually interested in. An antique writing journal, some glass earrings, and a massage at a local spa. They weren't bid on yet, so I had a chance to win them. I was considering the journal as a gift for my father. If I could win it, it would make the perfect gift for the upcoming Christmas.

I chewed on my bottom lip as I looked into the small box containing the journal. It was leather bound with elegant aging script inside, and the information card stated it was from the eighteenth century. It was definitely something my Georgian Era enthusiast collector of a father would love.

I wanted Jane's opinion on the journal before I bid, though. She knew my father well since we'd grown up together. He'd basically adopted her as one of his own kids after her parents died a few years ago. She would know if it was the right gift.

I found her at the Monet painting still talking with the man from before. Her eyes were bright with excitement, and she had a look I only saw on her face while she was working. It was delighted bliss.

"Lizzie," she called to me as I approached. "I'd like you to meet Charles Bingley. He's an art fan. Charles, this is my roommate, Elizabeth."

The man held out his hand. He was tall and thin with reddish hair and an eager smile. He looked like something out of one of Jane's art books he was so handsome. His handshake was firm yet gentle, and there was a kind sparkle in his eyes.

"It's a pleasure to meet you," I told him. Something about his name tickled my memory. "Wait, are you the Charles Bingley that just bought those old hotels?"

"Guilty," he admitted. He glanced around the hotel. "Don't tell the competition I'm here."

I chuckled, already liking him. "You wouldn't also happen to be renting a penthouse near 96th by any chance, would you?"

"How did you guess?" he asked. His green eyes were surprised but happy. "I only just moved in."

"That's my building," Jane told him, her smile getting bigger. Her hand fluttered near her necklace with excitement. "You moved into my building."

Charles grinned wider. "Then I think I made an excellent choice. We can have more discussions about Monet. I'd love to get your perspective on Degas addition to the field."

Jane grinned and made a small excited noise. She was usually so reserved with her emotions that just that giggle and smile was the equivalent of jumping up and down and whooping with joy.

"If you like art, Jane will talk your ear off," I told him. "She's a painter herself."

"What? You didn't tell me that," Charles said, turning back to Jane.

"I dabble," she replied with a small shrug. "I restore art. Sometimes, I paint."

"Painting is my real love, too." Charles looked at her like he'd won the lottery. He had to shake himself slightly so he could stop staring at her. "Unfortunately, I'm not very good at it yet, so I can't quit my day job."

"If what I've read is correct, you happen to be very good at your day job," I said, trying to keep the conversation going. If I didn't say something, the two of them were going to just stare and smile at one another. "You own a hotel chain and several nightclubs."

Charles nodded. "Yes. But, I would love just to paint."

"I'd love that, too," Jane told him. She blushed hard. "I mean, someday, I'd like just to paint."

Charles' eyes went back to her, and it was like they were the only two people in the entire room. I could have sworn I heard Cupid's arrow whoosh past me on it's way to the two of them. They both grinned at one another.

"Did you see the Loiseau?" Charles asked Jane.

"I did, but I'd love to hear your thoughts on it," Jane replied breathlessly. I knew it wasn't just a line. She really did want to hear what he had to say.

I chuckled and took a quiet step back. I was forgotten by the two of them, and I was very okay with that. Jane looked happier than I'd seen in a long time. She looked comfortable walking around with Charles, despite the fact that I knew she didn't like crowds much.

She was lost to her art, and he was right there with her. The crowd didn't matter here.

I watched them for a moment, seeing the attraction between them grow with every word. It was beautiful and incredibly sweet. I could wait to get Jane's opinion on the journal. I didn't want to interrupt her falling in love.

I gave the happy couple one more smile before turning and walking back to the party. I wanted another drink and to see what else the party had to offer. Besides, I needed to check on Lydia and make sure she hadn't terrorized the rich and famous too much.

Chapter 3

I found Lydia at the bar having a great time with a man. She was flirting and giggling with him for everything she was worth. I wanted to warn her, but she waved me away before I could get close. I just hoped that she knew the man she was flirting with wasn't rich and famous. He was the other hospital winner of tickets to tonight's event. He worked on the floor below me as a transport technician. If she was hoping he was her ticket to fame and fortune, she was in for a surprise.

I picked up a fresh drink while she glared daggers at me to leave her alone. She mouthed the words, "go away," leaving no doubt that she didn't want my interference. I gave her a friendly wave and headed off to see the rest of the party.

It was amazing. There was a live band, amazing food, free drinks, and beautiful people everywhere. For the night, I felt like I'd been transported to a different world. I rubbed elbows with the rich and famous. I found myself having a wonderful conversation with an older woman who owned my favorite restaurant and her husband who ran my favorite shopping center.

It was a wonderful party.

"Just an announcement folks," the singer of the band called out. "The silent auction will be ending in ten minutes. If you want to make some last minute bids on some amazing items, now is the time to do so. Remember, all proceeds go to these amazing hospitals."

I thought about the journal. It wouldn't hurt to see if anyone else had bid on it. If someone had, then I would find something else for my dad, but if it was available, that journal was mine. The more I thought about it, the more perfect I realized it would be for him.

I said goodbye to my conversation and hurried over to the journal. I found that no one had bid on it and I grinned. It was a little more than I wanted to spend, but it was mine for the taking. I quickly wrote down my name with my bid, feeling confident that I would win.

I felt rather proud of myself as I stood back and waited for the end of bidding so I could claim my prize. I could already imagine my dad's face when he opened the gift. His eyes would go wide, and his jaw would drop. He might even cry. It was going to be amazing.

Out of the corner of my eye, I noticed someone writing a bid on my journal. Not only that, it was the jerk who ran into me earlier at the bar. Of all the people at the party, *he* had to bid on my item. My hand tightened around my empty martini glass, and I had to stop and take a deep breath.

Once he set the pen down, I was there. The journal was now way above what I should spend on a gift, but I didn't care. It was a matter of principle now. I couldn't let that jerk take my father's present. I signed my name with a flourish.

"Lizzie, there you are," Jane called to me as I finished signing. There were only a few minutes left in the auction, and the jerk was off bidding on a different item. I felt confident I had won. He wouldn't come back in the last few minutes and steal my dad's journal.

Jane still stood next to the Loiseau. Her cheeks were flushed with excitement and she still only had her first drink in her hand. I wondered if she had ever even left this room, or if she and Charles had just stood here and talked about the paintings for the entire party. While that sounded terrible to me, I knew that it would be Jane's ideal way to spend the evening.

"Where's Charles?" I asked, looking around for her handsome conversation partner.

"He's getting me a drink and looking for his friend," she replied. "He'll be back in a moment. Did you find anything to bid on?"

"An antique journal," I told her. "And I'm pretty sure I've won it."

"Oh, that would be perfect for your dad," Jane agreed. "I know you've been looking for something special for him. I'm sure he'll love it."

"I think so, too," I replied. Jane's approval made me even more glad I had bid on it. "Did you bid on anything?"

Jane laughed and carefully pushed a blonde strand of hair back into place. "No, but more because Charles and I just talked. I completely lost track of time with him."

I grinned and gave my beautiful friend a hug. I couldn't have been happier for her. If she met someone who shared her passion for art, then I considered tonight a roaring success. The fact that her new friend happened to be very wealthy was just a perk.

"Bidding has now ended," someone announced. I grinned. That journal was mine.

"I'll be right back," I told Jane. "I'm going to check on my fancy journal. I have to figure out how to wrap it."

"Gold ribbon and red wrapping," Jane informed me with a smile. "And let me make the card. You always butcher the letters."

I laughed as I walked over to the table with the journal, feeling light and happy. Until I looked at the bidding sheet, that is.

My name was no longer last.

His was.

William Darcy.

He stole my journal.

The dirt-bag must have come back while I was talking to Jane and outbid me. All my dreams of surprising my father and making him smile vanished. I was no longer the hero of Christmas. I was a loser.

I stomped back to Jane, nearly tripping over my heels in the long skirt of my fancy gown.

"You okay?" Jane asked, taking one look at my face.

"I didn't win it," I said simply.

"Oh, Lizzie, I'm so sorry," Jane replied. "I'm sure you'll think of something else for your dad."

"Yeah." I sighed. "If not, I can always resort to my classic mug and funny t-shirt gift."

Jane patted my shoulder and gave me a commiserating look.

"Jane, I'd like to introduce you to someone," Charles said, coming up beside her. He was smiling, and his cheeks were just as flushed with pleasure as Jane's. If anything could make me feel better, it was that. He liked her as much as she liked him.

"Of course," Jane agreed, her own smile getting brighter.

"Jane, this is my friend, William Darcy," Charles announced. He turned and motioned to the man who stole my journal. "Will, this is Jane and her roommate, Elizabeth."

It took everything I had not to slap his smug face.

But, then I decided to be the bigger person. Maybe he had a father that loved antiques as well. Perhaps he was a collector and had finally found his dream piece. If the journal were going to a good home, I could bare it.

Maybe he wasn't evil. I could at least give him the benefit of the doubt now that I had to meet him.

"It's nice to meet you both," the man replied. He spoke with a British accent that immediately made me think of a Bond villain. It probably helped that he held himself like one too. He was all aloof and high and mighty.

"Likewise," I replied with as genuine a smile as I could muster. "I saw you won the antique journal. Congratulations, William."

"What?" Confusion crossed his handsome features. "And please, call me Mr. Darcy."

I did a small double take and felt like an admonished child. Apparently, we weren't on a first name basis despite being introduced as such. I didn't realize we were still in grade-school and he was the teacher.

"Okay, then, *Mr. Darcy*. The antique journal. Item number thirty-two," I explained, trying to remain patient. "You outbid me and won."

"Oh. That." He shrugged. His attention seemed to be elsewhere. "I just tried to buy up anything that wasn't selling. It's all for a good cause."

"You mean, you didn't want the journal?" I asked, my temper starting to rise.

"Why in the world would I want an antique journal?" he replied, looking at me like I was the crazy one.

"I wanted that journal," I told him. My face felt hot. "I bid on it. Twice."

"Then you should have bid higher," he told me flatly. "I'm very sorry, but that's just how it works."

My fingers clenched into a ball. Jane was giving me a death glare to behave and not cause a scene. I took a deep breath. We were in public and getting angry wasn't going to solve anything.

"Excuse me. I need to go check on my sister," I told him. I smiled and nodded politely to Jane and Charles before swiveling on my heels and walking out. I could feel them all looking at me. Mr. Darcy's eyes felt like hot lasers.

So, I walked as sexy as possible.

Stare away, Mr. Darcy, I said in my head. *Eat your heart out, because there is no way in heaven or hell that you get anywhere near me ever again.*

Chapter 4

*I*t took me less than five seconds to find my sister, because she was standing on a chair at the bar waving to Layla and calling out the actress' name.

The movie star was ignoring her and leaving the party. Lydia continued to shout, perilously teetering on the chair and looking like she might fall down at any moment.

I hurried over and pulled her down. Several people were staring. I thanked my lucky stars that none of my co-workers had won tickets because this was embarrassing. At least we would never have to see these rich people again after tonight.

"What are you doing?" Lydia slurred. She pushed me away, but not before I could smell the alcohol drenching her.

"Fix your dress," I hissed at her. "You're embarrassing yourself."

Lydia looked down at her dress to see her bra poking out of the top. She giggled and tugged her strapless dress back up to cover it. "It's not that big of a deal, Lizzie."

"What are you doing?" I asked her. I leaned over and

motioned to the bartender for a drink. I needed one. No, I needed three.

"Getting famous," Lydia replied. "I want another drink, too."

"No, you're cut off," I told her. The bartender nodded as he handed me a martini. I chugged it as soon as he set it down, ignoring the burning sensation down my throat. I motioned for another.

Lydia pouted. "I'm not that drunk," she said, trying to sit down on a chair and missing. She caught herself before falling too much. "Besides, I have great news."

"That's fantastic," I told her. The bartender handed me a new martini, looking at little hesitant this time. I took a delicate sip, and he looked less worried. I turned back to Lydia, giving her my full attention. "Okay, what's your news?"

"I found a talent scout. He likes me, and I'm going to be in all kinds of commercials," Lydia announced. "That's him in the blue suit."

She pointed directly at the transport assistant from downstairs.

"You mean the guy with the man-bun and the suit jacket that's too big?" I asked. I took another delicate sip of my drink.

"Yeah. He told me he could get me in all kinds of commercials," Lydia told me proudly. "He's going to take me back to his place, and we're going to discuss what I want to do first."

I took a nice long sip of my drink. It was soothing, and I was going to need more at the rate this night was going.

"That's Eddie. He's an orderly on the fourth floor of my hospital. He is the other employee who won tickets to tonight. He is not a talent scout," I told her, trying to use a gentle voice. "Unless you are laying on a gurney and need transport, he's not going to help your career."

"What?" Lydia's mouth opened in shock. She looked back and forth between Eddie and me in shock. "Why didn't you tell me?"

"I tried. Remember when you shooed me away?"

Her eyes went wide.

"You should have tried harder," she chastised me. She crossed her arms and pouted. "Well, I'm not going home with him now."

"That's probably a good idea," I agreed. She rolled her eyes at me before trying to stand up and nearly falling down.

"Now who is going to make me famous?" she mumbled, tripping over her own feet as she took a step away from me. I barely managed to catch her. She was totally drunk.

"No one. We're going home," I told her. "You'll have to find fame another time."

"No!" she shouted. People turned and looked at her. "This is supposed to be my big break!"

"No, this is supposed to be a fun party for the three of us," I replied, keeping my voice low. "This was supposed to be a fun night out, remember?"

Lydia crossed her arms and pouted.

"Look, it's time to go home," I told her gently. I motioned to the bar. "They're closing the bar."

She looked over to see the bartender put up a small "closed" sign and walk away. The pout on her face got larger. She let out a loud hiccup.

"I don't feel so good," she told me. I sighed and quickly finished my martini

"Come sit over here by the door, and I'll go get Jane and our jackets," I said gently. She followed me on wobbly legs to the lobby of the hotel where she plopped down into an overstuffed chair looking utterly miserable.

I made sure she was going to stay in her chair before heading into the crowd to find Jane. Looking back at Lydia, she looked more likely to pass out in her chair than throw up, so I knew I had a little bit of time. I headed back to the silent auction area where I had last seen Jane.

The lobby was crowded as people prepared to leave the party, and it took me a while to navigate through it. I was almost to the ballroom where I hoped to find Jane when I got stuck behind a wealthy woman looking for her fur coat. I couldn't find a way past, so I had to wait until she moved.

I saw Mr. Darcy and Charles walking through the lobby just ahead of me. It was hard to miss the two of them. Mr. Darcy stood out in a crowd. He was tall and incredibly handsome. His dark hair and blue eyes were just my type. It was a damn shame he was such an ass.

I laughed as I realized I called him Mr. Darcy when thinking of him. Even in my head, he was now *Mr. Darcy*. He was too pretentious for me to call him anything but that.

I could hear Jane's voice in my head to give the man a second chance. Jane was all about second chances. I sighed. He did buy a bunch of items at the auction to benefit the hospital. He was helping raise funds, and I could appreciate that. I decided I could give him a second chance.

I took a step in his direction, trying to escape the crowd in front of me. I couldn't get close enough to join the two men though, but I couldn't help but overhear their conversation.

"I can't believe I'm going home alone tonight," Mr. Darcy said in his British accent. It managed to sound snooty and sad at the same time. He was definitely a James Bond villain.

"I can't believe it either," Charles agreed, shuffling

slightly to the side to make room for the crowd. "It's almost like you were stand-offish and rude."

I snickered slightly.

"Actually, I can't believe that you aren't taking that pretty blonde home," Mr. Darcy replied, ignoring Charles' quip. "I think she was on your arm the entire night."

"Jane?" Charles' smile was evident in his voice even though I was behind them. "I want to take it slow and do it right. I think there's a future with her."

"Are you bloody serious?" Mr. Darcy asked, turning and looking at his friend. "You sound like a bad romance novel."

Charles just chuckled. "Yes, I know you're laughing at me, but I don't care." He shrugged. "I like her, and I'm not going to rush her into bed just because I can."

Mr. Darcy shook his head. "That's a mistake. You know you-"

"I know very well what I can do," Charles cut him off. "Besides, I'm not the one striking out and unhappy about it. I'm very happy with how my night went."

"You're not getting shagged either," Mr. Darcy replied.

"I want it to be special," Charles replied. "That's the point. I'm not making the same mistake twice."

I couldn't see their faces, but Mr. Darcy just sighed. "I don't get you sometimes. You could have any girl here, and you're going home alone."

"It's not just about shagging," Charles replied. Even though he was American, he mimicked Mr. Darcy's accent when he said 'shagging'. "It's about connection."

"You seem to think that's important." Mr. Darcy looked over at Charles like he was slightly insane. "I don't need connection."

Charles sighed.

"What about Jane's roommate? Elizabeth?" Charles

asked. "Maybe you could ask her for drinks and see where it goes. She's your type. From what Jane told me, I think you two would get along well."

"My type? You mean money hungry?" Mr. Darcy countered.

My eyes widened. No one had ever called me money hungry before.

"Ouch," Charles replied, turning to look at his friend. "I didn't get that from her. What's your problem with her?"

"She's wearing a designer gown she can't afford and bidding on items just for attention," Mr. Darcy explained. "She's just here to meet a rich husband, so she doesn't have to work her meaningless job. I doubt there's a brain cell in her head that actually functions."

I stopped cold, my jaw hitting the floor. Every word out of his mouth was wrong. The gown was a rental, so I could definitely afford it. I had only bid on items I could afford. I had no desire to meet my husband. I loved my job as a nurse, and I had a freaking master's degree.

My first impression of him was dead on. He was an ass.

"Wow." Charles stopped and looked at his friend. Even from behind them, I could see the disbelief on his face. "Don't hold back. Please, tell me how you really feel."

"Did you see her younger sister?" Mr. Darcy continued. "Looking for fame and money. The movie star had to leave early to avoid her. She was drunkenly screaming at the bar like a lunatic. The whole family is nothing but trouble."

And he had to insult my sister? His second chance flew out the window like a canary being chased by a cat.

"You sound like Catherine," Charles told him with a snicker. "Next you'll say something about them being beneath your bloodline."

"I do not sound like my Chief Operations Officer," Mr. Darcy replied. "I sound nothing like her."

"She's just here to meet a rich husband, so she doesn't have to work her meaningless job," Charles repeated, but in a high-pitched, British, old-lady voice.

The way Mr. Darcy glared at Charles told me it was a good impression. I was too angry to laugh at it, though. The crowd moved forward, and I was pushed a couple of steps closer to the two of them.

"It doesn't mean she's wrong," Mr. Darcy told Charles. "Besides, you're just in a good mood, or you'd see it too."

"I am in a good mood," Charles agreed.

"See? Drunk on love. You found the prettiest girl here, and she happens to like art," Mr. Darcy continued. "You're so twitterpated that you don't even care that you're leaving alone for the night."

"She knew about abstract impressionism," Charles said, sighing happily. "And I don't care what you think. She made my night."

Mr. Darcy snorted. Somehow, he managed to make that sound stuck-up too.

"Some things are worth waiting for," Charles informed him. "She's one of them."

"You can wait for things then," Mr. Darcy replied. "I get what I want, when I want it. I won't be waiting like a lovesick fool for any woman."

"She noticed the brush strokes," Charles said, completely ignoring Mr. Darcy. He walked like he was on clouds rather than tiled floors.

"Good," Mr. Darcy said. "Perhaps now you can take her to those awful art shows, and I can stay home."

Charles laughed. "No way. I still need some way to torture you."

Mr. Darcy shook his head and chuckled. "Of course you do."

"I'm so happy," Charles said with a soft sigh. He looked over at his friend. "I wish there were someone that could make you this happy."

"Not going to art shows might do it," Mr. Darcy told him. "Besides, I don't need love."

The crowd moved forward, and I was now right behind them. I wished I didn't have to listen in on this conversation anymore, but with the crowd the way it was, there was nowhere else for me to get to the auction room to find Jane.

"Everyone needs love," Charles told Mr. Darcy. "Even you."

"No, I need to get laid," Mr. Darcy replied. He rubbed the bridge of his nose. "I don't want it to mean anything."

"Then pick someone you don't care about," Charles replied, exasperated.

Mr. Darcy shrugged. "Maybe the flatmate will work for the night. She looks like she'd be up for a shag. She'd probably do it just for the bragging rights. It'll be easy, if terrible."

White hot rage flowed through me. I didn't stop to think. Anger propelled me forward.

I walked right over to him and slapped his face.

"How's that for a bragging right?" I spat. My hand stung as a red mark grew on Mr. Darcy's cheek. Charles' eyes went wide. "You don't know anything about me."

Mr. Darcy's hand went to his cheek. He hadn't even touched it for two seconds when two giant security guards were suddenly on either side of him giving me death glares. I wasn't even sure how they'd gotten through the crowd. One of them reached forward and grabbed my arm. His grip was iron.

It was a good thing I was still angry, or I would have been terrified.

"Ma'am, you're going to leave. Now," the big guard informed me. I tried to pull out of his grip, but he wasn't letting go.

"I was just on my way out," I said, hoping I sounded calmer than I felt. "I just need to get my roommate. She's right there."

Jane magically appeared at the far end of the lobby just as I needed her. She had all three of our jackets on her arm, but she hadn't seen the guards or me yet.

The guards looked at Mr. Darcy to see what he wanted them to do.

"Let her go," he said, gingerly touching the red welt on his cheek. "Just as long as she doesn't hit me again."

"Roommate and out. We're watching." The vice-like grip left me, and they stood with arms crossed behind Mr. Darcy.

I was tempted to hit him again just out of spite but had no desire to tangle with his massive bodyguards. So I just threw back my shoulders and raised my chin defiantly.

"You deserved it, you ass." I smoothed my dress and then turned and walked calmly to Jane as if it were my choice and not the guards' directions.

"There you are," Jane greeted me as soon as I got closer to her. "This place is a zoo."

"No kidding," I agreed. "I think I just met a couple of lions."

Jane gave me a strange look, but then just shook her head as she was used to me being weird.

"Guess what? Charles invited me to an art opening next week." Her eyes sparkled, and she grinned.

I thought of how happy he had sounded talking to Mr. Darcy about her and smiled. At least he seemed like a decent human being, even if his taste in friends was terrible.

"I'm so happy for you," I replied as we made our way across the lobby with our jackets.

"Why are you walking so fast?" Jane asked, picking up her skirt to keep up with me.

"Sorry, I have to get Lydia home. She's trashed," I explained. I heard a noise across the lobby that sounded suspiciously like someone vomiting. I stopped walking fast because there was no reason anymore. "And she's throwing up. Oh, and, I might have gotten myself kicked out of the party."

"What?" Jane paused for a second before catching up. "Actually, I'm not sure I even want to know."

"You can stay longer if you'd like," I told Jane as I wound my way around the crowd. "Charles really seems to like you."

"I like him," Jane replied with a smile. It was short lived. "But, you need all the help you can get with Lydia. Remember last time?"

I wanted to tell her that I didn't and that she could be with Charles tonight. But the vomiting noise was getting worse and drunk Lydia was a handful. I was going to need all the help I could get.

We made it across the last bit of the lobby to find Lydia still on her chair, but with a splatter of what looked like mostly Long Island Iced Tea in front of her.

"I couldn't help it," Lydia whimpered, wrapping her arms around her legs as she curled up in the chair.

I ran to the bathroom to grab some paper towels. Luckily, the lobby was clearing out, so it didn't take me very long. I called to the front desk that we needed a cleanup, and they told me they were already on it. I came back to find Jane taking care of Lydia and making sure that no one stepped in anything.

I went to work cleaning up the mess. It was a good thing I was a nurse and knew how to handle this kind of thing. Sometimes, taking care of my sister was exhausting.

"Jane, there you are," Charles said, coming up to greet her.

"Watch out," I warned, and he stopped short. Mr. Darcy came up behind him, and they both grimaced at the mess.

"Jane, can I call you tomorrow?" Charles asked. "I know you're busy now."

Jane grinned. "I'd like that."

"Okay." A smile lit up Charles' face like the Fourth of July. It was absolutely the most adorable thing I had ever seen. "Tomorrow then."

Jane just sat there smiling at him, and he just stood there smiling at her. It was so sweet and innocent that it felt almost silly. It reminded me of being on the playground the first time someone admitted they had a crush.

Mr. Darcy cleared his throat and gave his friend a gentle push on the shoulder. Charles waved as the two of them walked off. I looked up just as Mr. Darcy looked back.

His eyes met mine. His expression was unreadable, yet it made my stomach do flip-flops. I couldn't help it, but I felt stupid. I felt like I didn't measure up to his standards. I didn't understand how I could feel like this, since I didn't care about him or what he thought of me. I didn't have to measure up to him at all. I didn't like him, and I certainly didn't care what he thought.

Yet, somehow, I couldn't take my eyes off him as he walked away.

Chapter 5

*J*ane waltzed around the kitchen, humming a happy tune to herself the next morning when I woke up. She was walking on air, and I couldn't help but smile as I watched her.

She was as twitterpated as Charles had been.

I went to the coffee pot to find it empty. The bag of coffee next to it was empty as well.

"Where's the coffee?" I asked, opening a cabinet to look for more.

"We're out," Jane said, still dancing around the kitchen with a goofy-happy smile on her face.

"And you're still happy?" I asked. "With no coffee? He must be a heck of a guy."

Jane grinned. "He texted me this morning. We're discussing watercolors."

I shook my head. Only Jane would be over the moon about discussing watercolors at eight in the morning with no coffee in sight.

"Jane, I need coffee. I need caffeine," I told her. "I'm

going to order some from the cafe. Want to come with me to get it?"

Jane spun around the kitchen to pick up my phone. She curtsied as she handed it to me. I wished I could be in that good of a mood without coffee. "Make sure to order one for Lydia," she reminded me.

I chuckled and opened up the phone app for our local coffee shop. It was just down the block, so if we ordered now, by the time we got there, it would be ready. I put in our traditional to-go orders and put on a pair of jeans. I kept my pajama top on since I'd have my sweatshirt over it anyway. It wasn't like we were going to run into anyone I needed to impress.

I threw on my sweatshirt and checked outside. It was early November, so the sweatshirt should be enough to keep me warm. Besides, we weren't going to be outside very long. Jane had a light jacket on as we left the apartment and headed to the elevator. Somehow, she managed to look put-together and elegant without any effort at all. I looked like a comfortable train wreck.

Jane giggled and grinned at her phone as we stepped into the elevator.

"Watercolors?" I asked, smiling at her.

Jane just beamed at me.

"You like him," I told her, pressing the elevator button for the ground floor. This was the happiest I had seen her in a long time.

"I do," she agreed with a happy sigh. She bit her lip and looked over at me. "Do you think he likes me?"

I thought back to the conversation I had overheard the night before.

"He's talking about watercolors at eight in the morning,"

I told her. "And, I don't think he spoke to another person except you all night. He definitely likes you."

Jane blushed as she grinned. She put her phone in her pocket as we stepped out of the elevator and out of our building.

"It's nice that he's rich, too," I commented, looking up at our building toward the penthouse. I wondered if he was up there, smiling and giggling at Jane's messages.

"That has nothing to do with it," Jane assured me with a glare. She couldn't hold the angry look for long, though. "It is nice to know that he can afford my expensive art tastes, though."

I laughed and bumped her shoulder. "That is definitely a perk."

"Did you know he's been to Paris three times?" she asked. "Do you know what I would do to go to Paris? The art they have there..."

"I know what you'd do," I told her. She looked over at me, waiting. "You'd do him."

Jane made an exasperated noise and rolled her eyes at me.

"And what about you?" Jane asked, changing the subject. "I saw you talking to William Darcy last night." She waggled her eyebrows at me. "I know you like tall, dark, and handsome."

"Him?" I scoffed. "Ugh."

"What? Really?" Jane shook her head. "Charles said he was his best friend. He had only nice things to say about him. I thought you'd like him."

"He said those nice things because Mr. Darcy is *his* friend," I told her. "Did I not tell you what happened last night with him?"

Jane shook her head. "You were going to, but Lydia was

too much of a handful. I could have sworn you said something like you got kicked out, but that doesn't make any sense."

"I slapped Mr. Darcy," I informed her.

"What?" Jane stopped short and stared at me. "You slapped him?"

I nodded.

"He called me a gold-digger in a dress I couldn't afford and bidding on items for attention. Then he said I looked like I would be up for a *shag* just to be able to brag about it," I told her. Somehow, I managed to imitate his British accent on the word 'shag' as well as Charles had last night. "So, I slapped him. Not my best moment, but it felt right."

Jane stared at me open-mouthed.

"He's an ass," I explained. I gave her a gentle push to keep walking. I wanted my coffee.

"Okay, two things. One, why do you keep calling him Mr. Darcy?" Jane asked, finally moving her feet again.

"He told me to. I called him William, and he corrected me. He is forever now Mr. Darcy," I explained.

"Okay." Jane took a deep breath. "And second, do you know who he is?"

I shrugged. "Some British rich guy with no class?"

"You don't know who he is?" She grinned. "Let me savor knowing something that you don't for just a moment. This never happens."

She closed her eyes and took a deep, contented breath. It was my turn to roll my eyes this time.

"So, who is he?"

"He's the biggest name in the airline industry. He owns and runs Oceanic Airlines. He's worth billions of dollars, and you slapped him in the face," Jane informed me with a chuckle. "Nice going."

I stopped short and stood in front of the coffee shop just blinking for a moment.

"Are you serious?" I asked her, my heart stalling out a little bit. "I slapped a billionaire?"

Jane nodded. "Yup."

I shook my head and went to open the door to the coffee shop. The smell of freshly roasted beans was heaven.

"That does explain the bodyguards, then. I can't believe he has all that money and still is a terrible person," I said to Jane.

"Who is a terrible person?"

I spun to see Charles come up beside us. I was suddenly happy I hadn't said Mr. Darcy's name.

"No one," I quickly lied. "Just speaking in generalities. Work thing."

"Okay," he replied with a small head shake. Then his smile focused on Jane, and my words were forgotten. "Jane. What a wonderful surprise to see you here."

The way he said her name held such warmth that even I felt it.

"I didn't know you were getting coffee," Jane replied. She was blushing hard as she smiled at him.

"It's the closest coffee to me now. Join us. We have a table," Charles said, motioning to a spot on the side of the shop.

And just guess who was sitting there.

Mr. Darcy.

Of course he was.

I looked down and noticed a new stain on my sweatshirt. Plus, now I had no makeup on, and my hair was up in the messiest ponytail ever. I didn't know why it bothered me so much that he was going to see me like this. This was more my natural look, and besides, I didn't like him. I shouldn't care what he thought.

Luckily, I had an escape route.

"Actually, we pre-ordered. I'm just going to grab mine and go. I need to bring some back for my sister," I explained. "Jane can stay, though."

Charles grinned at Jane before looking back at me. "Of course. How is your sister feeling?"

"Hungover and a bit embarrassed," I told him. The first part was true, even if the second part was a stretch. I couldn't remember the last time I'd seen Lydia embarrassed.

Jane and Charles walked with me up to the to-go counter. All I had to do was grab my sister's coffee, and then I could leave the restaurant without having to say a word to Mr. Darcy. I could merely wave and politely disappear before he could find out I still had my pajama shirt on and hadn't brushed my teeth yet this morning.

"Are you Elizabeth?" the employee asked as we came up.

I nodded. "That's me. I should have three coffees."

"We're really sorry," the barista said. "Our machine needs to be reset, so it's going to be a few extra minutes. Coffee's on us. I'm really sorry about the wait."

And my easy escape vanished just like that.

"Come sit with us," Jane told me. "We'll wait with Charles.

Charles just beamed at Jane, seeing no one else in the world but her. He motioned over to the table again. "Please, come have a seat."

I took a deep breath and let it out slowly. The coffee would only be a couple of minutes. Maybe I'd get lucky, and he wouldn't even bother to look up from his phone.

Jane took the seat across from Charles, which of course

meant I was across from Mr. Darcy. He looked up from his phone as I sat down, his expression unchanging.

I fidgeted for a moment, his eyes on me. I had no makeup on, so maybe he didn't recognize me.

"You're not going to hit me again, are you?" he asked after a moment.

"Not as long as you watch what you say," I replied.

There was a long, awkward silence. Next to us, Jane and Charles were having an animated discussion about some art thing that I didn't understand. There was no way for me to join in on their conversation. I was stuck with Mr. Darcy.

I fiddled with the string on my sweatshirt and sent a silent plea to the universe to fix the coffee machine as quickly as possible. This would be awkward regularly, but I hadn't had a single cup of coffee yet, which just made it all the worse.

He typed one more thing into his phone before setting it down and looking me over. His eyes were so blue and sharp. I felt naked under his gaze. For a moment, I wondered what it would feel like to be naked in front of him for real before remembering that despite his good looks, he was an absolute jerk and I had vowed never to even think of sleeping with him.

"I'm really sorry about last night," I finally said, trying to break the tension. "How's your cheek?"

"Fine," he replied. He turned to show me that there wasn't a mark.

I should have hit him harder.

"I was actually curious, though," he continued. "Why were you at the fundraiser? What's your affiliation with the hospital?"

I decided to ignore the implication that I obviously

didn't belong at the fancy party. It was true, but that didn't take any of my indignation away.

"I work at St. Austen's. I'm an RN in the Cardiac ICU," I explained. Then I remembered how he said I hated my dead-end job, so I added, "We actually just won an award for being one of the best ICUs in the nation."

"The best?" He raised his eyebrows. "Even against St. George Hospital?"

St. George's Hospital was the main competition for my hospital. They were the two hospitals that had teamed up to run the fundraiser.

"St. George is known for their cancer research. St. Austen is known for our amazing cardiac outcomes," I explained. "I'm sure their CICU is good, ours is just better."

He made a thoughtful noise and took a sip of his coffee. He smiled slightly like he was making fun of me.

"What?" I asked, trying to keep my temper.

"Nothing," he said, shaking his head. I gave him a disbelieving look, and he smiled. "You surprise me. Not many people contradict me." He paused. "Or hit me for that matter."

"I am sorry about that," I told him. "I don't usually hit people."

"Why the ICU?" he asked, ignoring my apology again.

"What do you mean?"

"Everyone has a reason for the work they're in," he explained. "Why the ICU and not surgery or pediatrics?"

I thought about giving him a flippant answer. I thought about giving him the answer that it was just what was open when I applied, but I didn't. I decided to be honest with him.

"My grandmother," I told him. "She's the reason I'm a nurse in the first place. She was a nurse, and I wanted to be just like her. She was this vibrant, sassy woman that loved the hell out of my sister and me. She had a heart attack while I was in nursing school."

"I'm sorry to hear that," he replied politely.

"I spent a lot of time with her in the ICU. I knew then that it was where I was supposed to be," I continued.

"I imagine she's proud of you," he said. It almost sounded sincere.

"I hope so. She died a year after I graduated with my master's degree."

"I'm sorry," he said. It sounded more sincere this time.

"So, now you've heard my life story," I replied, not liking the way his eyes softened when he looked at me. I didn't want his pity. "What about you? Why airplanes?"

"I inherited the business," he said with a shrug.

"But you could have done anything you wanted," I told him. "If you didn't want to run the company, you could have sold it or made yourself just a figurehead so you wouldn't have to do the hard parts."

"Who says I haven't done just that?" he asked, looking rather pleased with himself.

"The fact that you're doing business at eight in the morning on a Saturday," I replied, motioning to his phone. "Plus, you keep checking the news channel in the corner like your life depends on it. You obviously care about your business."

A flicker of a smile touched his face. "Is that so?"

"Besides, everyone has a reason for the work they're in," I quoted back to him, accent and all.

He took a sip of coffee to hide the small smile I had earned. "It was my father's company. My family expects me to do it. It's our family tradition, but even then, I couldn't let anyone else run it."

"So we're both in our line of work because of family," I

said with a smile. We had something in common. "I love my work. Do you enjoy yours?"

He frowned. "It's my life."

"Okay," I replied after a moment. So much for making a connection. I looked over at the coffee counter to see they were still working on our order. No coffee yet. "So, what else do you do?

"What do you mean?" he asked with a frown.

"What hobbies do you have?" I asked. "I personally like to go dancing. I like going to Jane's art shows and my sister's off-Broadway plays. And I mean, really *really* off-Broadway plays."

He nodded. "I go flying with Charles," he replied.

"You own an airline and flying is your fun?" I asked. If that wasn't a workaholic, then I wasn't sure what else qualified.

"I don't have time for other distractions," he informed me. "My business comes first. Excuse me. I need to reply to this email. It's my COO."

"COO?"

"Chief Operations Officer," he replied. "My aunt Catherine runs the day-to-day. She has for years."

And he picked up his phone and quickly typed something in, completely ignoring me.

"Oh." I wasn't sure quite how to reply to that. I folded my hands in my lap, unsure of what to say next. Apparently, we didn't have as much in common as I thought.

"Your coffee is ready, by the way," he informed me, not looking up from his phone. I looked over to see the barista setting three cups out on the counter.

"Oh, thank you," I told him, rising from my chair.

"You're welcome to stay longer if you'd like," he said,

looking up and locking me in the blue tractor beam of his gaze.

I wasn't sure what to think of that. Now he was polite? After the things he said last night? We were having a nice conversation, but it wasn't exactly riveting.

"Um, thanks," I replied. "But I really should get this coffee up to my sister."

"Of course. She must have a hangover," he said with a small nod before going back to his phone.

I shook my head a little before putting my hand on Jane's shoulder. It took me a moment to get her attention.

"Jane? Are you staying?" I asked her. "I'll go grab your coffee and bring it back if you are."

"That would be wonderful," Jane replied, barely looking away from Charles. "Thank you."

I went over and picked up the three drinks and brought them back over to the table. I set Jane's down beside her, and she looked up at me with a giant grin.

"Charles has invited us out tonight," Jane explained. "To Lux. The new dance club."

"I thought that place was impossible to get into right now," I replied. Lux was the hottest new dance scene in the city.

"I own it," Charles explained. "Well, partial owner. I need to make an appearance, and it would be wonderful to have you. Bring your sister if you'd like. William and I need beautiful women on our arms."

"Oh, wow." I looked over at Jane to see her mouth the word, "please." I was rather surprised by that as she usually hated dance clubs and the crowds that came with them. I gave her a questioning look, and she nodded toward Charles. She wanted to go because he had asked her.

"Please come," Mr. Darcy said. I looked over at him surprised that of all people he was asking.

"Um, sure," I replied, checking in once more with Jane. I couldn't believe she wanted this. Crowds made her anxious, and that's all a dance club was. She nodded again, so I smiled. "We'll all come."

Charles grinned. "Excellent."

"Okay." I wasn't sure what to do next, so I just picked up my and Lydia's coffees. "I'm just going to bring this home now. It was nice to see you both. Thank you for letting us sit at your table."

"Of course," Charles said with a smile, his eyes going back to the blushing Jane. Mr. Darcy simply gave an elegant nod.

I turned and left, feeling incredibly awkward. I was not expecting Mr. Darcy to be half so civil. I opened the door to leave and glanced back, finding that Mr. Darcy was still watching me. I instinctively smiled before hurrying out the door.

I had no idea what we were in store for tonight, but I did know that at least Lydia would be pleased.

Chapter 6

The lights of New York City sparkled in the dark sky instead of stars as we left our building and found a limo waiting for us. Lydia squealed with delight and clapped her hands as soon as she saw it, and even Jane looked impressed. It wasn't every day that we got to take a limo to a fancy nightclub.

The driver opened the door as we approached. Charles and Mr. Darcy were waiting for us inside the limo. Charles grinned as we got in. Mr. Darcy was talking on his phone.

Jane sat next to Charles. Lydia was the next in, which meant that I had to sit next to Mr. Darcy. He had dressed for the club and looked sexy as sin. He wore dark pants with a matching dress jacket. A crisp white button dress shirt peeked out from underneath his jacket, but he'd left it unbuttoned, giving him an easy, devilish look. If I didn't know that his personality was not as handsome, I would have been very attracted to him.

I, of course, did my best to ignore him as he hung up the phone. There was no way I was going to tell him he looked good. His ego was already too big.

"You all look amazing," Charles remarked as the car started moving forward.

Jane blushed. Jane was showing off her long legs and just enough cleavage to tease anyone who looked. Lydia had spent the afternoon convincing her it was a good idea to look sexy.

"They're designer dresses," Lydia announced. She was wearing a tiny little dress that left very little to the imagination. Mine was sweetheart cut and short, but more fun than overtly sexy.

"They're rentals," I added. Lydia glared at me, but I wasn't about to get called a gold-digger again because I was wearing a dress I couldn't afford. "A way for us common folk to get our hands on designer clothes without spending a fortune."

"What a smart idea," Charles replied. "I've never heard of anything like that."

"It is smart, isn't it?" I replied but looked at Mr. Darcy. His jaw tightened, and it made me smile. Score one for me.

"So, Lux?" Jane said, changing the subject. "I've never been."

"Is anyone famous going to be there tonight?" Lydia asked, fluttering her eyelashes at the two men.

I glared at her from across the limo. Why did she have to make everything we did about becoming famous?

"What?" She gave me the most teenager shrug I'd seen in weeks.

"There will be some big names there," Charles interjected, trying to keep the mood light. " We just opened last week, so we're trying to keep the momentum up."

"You said you own the club?" Jane asked.

"It's one of my investments. I'm a silent partner since I'm not really known for my nightclubs. I'm more of a hotel guy," Charles explained. He smiled at Jane. "I hope you like it."

"I know I will," she assured him.

"If you ever need someone to be on promotional materials, I'm really photogenic," Lydia told him, fluttering her eyelashes.

"Thank you, Lydia," I replied. "I'm sure he'll keep you in mind."

I was going to have to talk with her. She couldn't just keep pressing everyone she met to make her famous. I knew it was just because it was her dream and she was motivated, but she needed to work on making it sound less skeezy.

"We're here," Mr. Darcy announced. It was the first thing he'd said all night.

Mr. Darcy was the first to exit the limo. He held out his hand to help me out, and I took it without thinking. His grasp was solid and firm, holding me safely as I stepped out onto the street. But there was more to it than that. His touch stayed with me, sending little jolts of desire up my arm and down my spine.

I looked up and into his blue eyes. His gaze caught me off balance, and it was a good thing he was holding my hand, or I would have fallen. I felt something awake inside of me, but judging from his face, he didn't feel the same.

He simply made sure I was steady before letting me go and helping my sister out of the limo. My fingers tingled from where he touched me as I waited for the others. I watched him, not seeing any sign that he'd felt the same connection I did.

I knew I was being ridiculous. He was an ass. He hated me, and I hated him. It had to be in my head that we'd connected. My body was just responding to the fact that he was incredibly sexy and just my type. That had to be it. It was all physical.

The line to get into Lux wrapped around the street corner and down the block. Men and women in tight black clothing and fancy shoes all stood out in the November cold waiting to get in.

But we walked right in the front door without even a pause. The two security guards nodded to Charles and pulled back the red-velvet ropes. Between the limo and the no wait time, I could see Lydia's attraction with being famous. Not that I was ever going to go to her extremes, but I could at least see the appeal.

A photographer was waiting inside and snapped our picture without warning. The flash made my eyes blur for a moment, but I managed to put on a smile for the next picture. Jane veered to my left, shying away from the camera as much as possible. Despite being model beautiful, she hated getting her picture taken. She said she always looked terrible and avoided photos as much as possible.

Lydia on the other hand, stood posing for the photographer for another three shots before I pushed her inside to follow Charles and the rest of the group.

The club was hopping. Blue and silver lights flashed and swung over the packed dance floor on the first level. A second level wrapped around the edges of the building, providing places to sit and drink and look down on the dancers below. We had to go through another set of velvet ropes to go up, which told me that the upstairs was VIP only.

Music pulsed with a heavy beat that made my body want to move as we walked up the open staircase. Everywhere people were dancing, drinking, and having a good time. I grinned as we walked, knowing that I was going to have a great time tonight. I was going to dance and enjoy myself here.

Charles led us to a large table on the second level that overlooked the dance floor. We could see everything from up here. The DJ spun in his booth and dancers writhed to his music below us. This was the best table in the entire place.

"Champagne?" Charles offered as we took our seats at the comfortable lounge table. The table was round and made of reflective glass, while two benches wrapped around it. The seats were velvety and helped insulate from the sound below us so we could hold a conversation. Two bottles of Dom Perignon were waiting for us. I nodded, completely impressed.

"Yes, please," Jane whispered. Her eyes were big as she took a glass in a shaky hand. Crowds were not her thing. She gave me a nervous smile as she took a big sip of her drink and tried to relax. Her idea of a good time would be a quiet restaurant or a romantic dinner at home.

She smiled at me. I knew she was trying to have a good time, but this was not her idea of a good time. She was here because she wanted to spend time with Charles, not because she wanted to dance in the crowd. I squeezed her hand.

"Charles, this is amazing," I said, taking a glass of champagne from him. "Thank you so much for bringing us."

"You are very welcome," he replied. He glanced over at Jane, and she did her best to give him a big smile. "I hope you like it."

"Very much," Lydia assured him. She looked pleased as a cat in a canary cage as she looked around. I could only imagine what she was thinking of doing next.

"A toast," Charles announced once everyone had their champagne. "To new friends."

Everyone, even Mr. Darcy, clinked their glasses together and repeated the words.

The photographer returned just as we finished our toast. She held up the camera this time, prepping us for another round of pictures. We all leaned in, except Jane, and smiled. The camera flashed, and the photographer frowned. She motioned to Jane to move in closer.

Jane sighed, put on her best smile and tried to fit in the picture. Even I knew that she was just going to look out of place with the fake smile and uncomfortable pose. The photographer took the picture and shrugged before walking off to take more photos. I hoped it didn't look too terrible, for Jane's sake. She hated pictures like that as it was.

"William, how is your sister?" Charles asked, leaning back and sipping his champagne. "I heard she might be coming to town soon."

Who the hell is William? I thought for a moment before remembering that Mr. Darcy had a first name. I just wasn't supposed to use it. I looked over to see a smile flicker across his normally serious face.

"She is coming in December," he replied. "She loves New York this time of year. I half suspect that's the only reason she's willing to leave London. That and to get away from our aunt."

"You have a sister?" Jane asked. "Older or younger?"

"Younger," he answered. He still had a smile on his face. "Her name's Georgiana."

"Does she work for your company?" Lydia asked. "If she's like you, you must have her on all your fliers."

His smile flickered and faded. "No, she's been ill."

"I'm sorry to hear that," I said. Those blue eyes came to

mine, and I found it hard to breathe again. How did he have such a strong effect on me?

"Thank you," he said. I had no idea how he did that to me. I hated his guts, yet one look from him and my body decided that was something we could get over.

"She's doing better now," Mr. Darcy continued, looking away and freeing me from his spellbinding gaze. "She wants to help with the company once she's stronger."

"Do you think she can do it?" I asked, half hoping he'd look at me like that again.

"What, work?" He took another sip of champagne, looking like the billionaire playboy that he was. "Once she's healthy enough, yes. Running a business, especially a multi-billion dollar one, isn't for the weak. It's hard work."

"I can attest to that," Charles agreed. "And mine's not even a billion dollars. Yet."

Mr. Darcy nodded. "There's not many that can do it and even fewer in her condition. I wouldn't and couldn't ask it of her."

I wanted to ask him what illness his sister had. Being a nurse, I was always curious to know more medically, but I knew a nightclub wasn't exactly the best place to ask. Besides, a sibling's health was personal. However, I didn't even get the chance to ask before a woman in a slinky black dress came up.

"Hi, William," she purred, leaning against the chair and smiling at him. How did she get to call him William and I didn't?

Then I realized the answer. She oozed sex. She was clearly what he had been looking to take home the night of the fundraiser. I could barely believe that Mr. Darcy thought this sexy woman and I were in the same class. She had curves I could only dream of.

Mr. Darcy looked up from his drink. "Yes?"

"Would you like to dance?" She fluttered her eyelashes and puffed her chest out a little bit. Someone was getting laid. Or rather, as the Brits said, shagged.

"I don't dance," he said flatly, turning away and sipping on his drink.

The woman blinked twice. She looked around the table, pausing at me for a moment before shrugging. "Oh. Okay then."

She waited a moment longer for Mr. Darcy to change his mind before sashaying off.

"You don't dance?" I asked Mr. Darcy, watching the girl who was made for dancing walk away. "It's a club. Everyone dances. That's kind of the point."

"I don't dance," he repeated.

"It's not hard," I told him. "You just move your feet to the beat."

"I didn't say that I *can't* dance," he told me, setting down his drink. "I said that I don't."

I took a sip of my champagne, feeling the bubbles against my nose. "She wanted more than just dancing on the dance floor. Considering what you said the night we met, I thought you'd be interested in someone like that."

I could have sworn his cheeks flushed, but it was probably just the flashing lights of the club.

"She's not looking for a *dance* partner," he said, stressing the word dance. "She's looking for a meal ticket. And I'm not interested in that."

"Really?" I set my drink down. "Do I need to repeat what you said about me?"

Mr. Darcy's jaw tightened. "Do you see who she moved onto? She isn't looking for a good time. She's looking for someone to pay her way."

I followed his gaze to the young woman who was now sitting at another VIP table. An older but attractive man in an expensive suit had his arm wrapped around her shoulder as he handed her a glass of what appeared to be expensive champagne.

"So?" I asked. "Why do you assume the worst? I see two people having fun. A dance doesn't mean she's going to steal all his money. She wants to dance and the people up here don't have partners. If I were looking for someone to dance with, I'd try up here too."

"And you wouldn't want a thing after? You wouldn't ask for expensive jewelry or lavish accommodations?"

"Do women usually ask that of you?" I asked. "Besides, what if they fall madly in love? She's in the VIP area. Maybe she's paying for *his* drinks. She knew you, so she's obviously not broke."

He looked at me with those serious eyes again, evaluating. I wondered if I said something stupid yet again.

"What?" I asked, waiting to be told I was wrong.

"You see the good in people," he replied. "I don't. For me, everyone wants something."

"Everyone wants to matter," I said. "For some, that means money, but for most people, it means they want a connection. To feel special. If you don't give people a chance, they can't surprise you with how good they can be."

He finished his glass of champagne, and I wasn't sure if he was ignoring my words or considering them. Given it was Mr. Darcy, my bet was on ignoring them. He'd already made it clear I was beneath him.

He reached for his phone and checked the screen.

"Excuse me," he said, rising from his seat. "Business calls."

He took his phone out and answered it, moving away from the music and toward a more quiet area of the club to talk. Given that he was friends with Charles, he was probably headed to the club's office. It seemed silly to come to a club at all if that was what he was going to do.

"Where's he off to?" Lydia asked, pouring herself a second glass of champagne.

"Business," I replied. "I admit, I work a lot, but that just seems excessive."

"I'm actually surprised he came tonight," Charles replied. "He has a big meeting tomorrow morning. His company is merging with another. It's rather touch-and-go at the moment."

"He came because he wanted to help you," Jane said. "He's a good friend."

"That he is," Charles agreed, patting her arm. "Would you like to dance?"

"No!" Jane blushed. "I mean, no thank you. Can we just stay up here?"

Charles looked down at the dancers below us and back to Jane. "Of course. How about another toast, then?"

The four of us clinked our glasses together again. "To a good time," we chorused.

"I want to dance," Lydia announced. She grabbed my hand, knowing that Jane hated crowds.

"Have another drink," I whispered to Jane as I stood up. "You're doing great."

Jane smiled meekly and gulped at her champagne. I was going to have to tell Charles not to take her to crowded places like this. It wasn't Jane's style, but I knew she would say yes to anything he offered. She wanted to be with him.

Lydia and I walked down the stairs and onto the

crowded dance floor. Halfway down, I looked back up at the table to see Mr. Darcy watching me.

I shrugged. He didn't want to dance anyway. He could just stay up there and do business. I was going to have some fun.

Chapter 7

*T*he crowd absorbed me, and the music became my world. Lydia was dancing with someone within seconds of hitting the dance floor. Knowing her, she'd either have the whole club dancing with her by the end of the night or have the entire security team throwing her out. I hoped it was the first. I could see enough bouncers that I wasn't worried about her safety. She was safe here in Charles Bingley's club.

I started dancing, letting the champagne and music loosen my hips. I wasn't anywhere near drunk, just tipsy and loose. I felt good, and I knew that in this dress, I looked good too. I was going to enjoy myself. It wasn't often that I got to dance.

Someone tapped my shoulder. Thinking I was in the way of a person trying to get by, I turned and prepared to move to the side. A short man in khakis and a polo shirt with a work logo stood unmoving in front of me.

"Can I help you?" I asked over the music when he didn't try to get past me.

"Do you want to..." The music drowned out his voice.

"I can't hear you," I told him, shaking my head and pointing to my ears.

"DO YOU WANT TO DANCE?" He yelled, enunciating every word.

"Um, sure," I told him, not wanting to be rude. It wasn't like I was dancing with anyone else.

He put his hands on my hips and stood at arm's length away. I didn't know what else to do with my hands except put them on his shoulders. It felt like an awkward middle school dance all over again.

"I'm Collins," he shouted over the music. "What's your name?"

"Lizzie," I replied. I already wished the song would come to an end. Shuffling my feet back and forth while he stood a good two feet away with his hands awkwardly on my hips was not fun dancing. We weren't even with the beat of the song.

"That's an odd name," he replied. "I've never met a Zizzy before."

"No, Lizzie, with an L," I told him.

"Zilly?"

"Yeah, sure. We'll go with that."

The next few moments felt like an eternity. Collins shuffled his feet directly opposite of the beat, making any movement feel completely out of place. Plus, we were the only couple in the entire club that had the middle school dance pose going. He kept trying to have a conversation, but with the music as loud as it was, that was impossible.

"Thank you," I told him, stepping away as soon as the music changed even a little bit.

"Would you like another?" He pursed his lips in what I assumed was an attempt at a sexy face. It was either that, or he was going to be sick.

"I'm good, thanks," I replied, taking a step back. "I'd like to dance around a bit. Thanks, though."

He nodded sharply and immediately went to another girl. She grinned at him.

"You're pretty cute," she cooed. "I'm Charlotte."

He grinned at her, and I quickly moved deeper into the crowd as he started his awkward dance routine with her. If the two of them were dancing, who was I to stand in the way of their happiness?

I KEPT DANCING across the dance floor, moving my hips and having fun. I could see Lydia out of the corner of my eye shaking her booty and having a great time. For once, I wasn't worried about her getting kicked out. She seemed to be behaving herself.

A cute man came up and started dancing with me. He was mid-height with blonde hair and a couple of tattoos peeking out from under his shirtsleeves. I offered my hand, and he spun me into him, putting his hands on my hips and moving with me to the music.

At first, the dance was fun. Cute-guy kept his hands on my hips, pulling me into his body and moving to the music. It was worlds away better than dancing with Collins, but then he started going too far. He grabbed my ass instead of my hips, and he didn't let me go as he thrust his pelvis into me.

I stepped away, no longer enjoying what was going on. I wanted to dance, not to be groped.

"Come on, baby," he said over the music, flashing me what I assumed was his best smile. He was no longer Cute-guy. He was now Cute-but-awful guy. "It's just for fun."

"I think I'm done," I said, turning to leave, but he grabbed my hand.

"Just another dance, baby," he cooed. "I'll behave. Until you don't want me to."

I tried to wrench my arm from his grasp, but he was much bigger and stronger than me. I wasn't sure what to do. Should I play nice until he let me go and then run? Should I kick him in the balls? Scream bloody murder?

"She said she's done," a strong voice said behind me. I turned to find Mr. Darcy out on the dance floor. For the first time since meeting him, I was glad to see him.

"Wait your turn," Cute-but-awful guy told him. He still had my wrist in his hand.

"No," Mr. Darcy said, putting his hand on my shoulder. He looked dangerous. "Either you leave now, or they help you out."

He nodded to the three muscle-bound bouncers in black watching them. Cute-but-awful guy dropped my wrist.

"You need to chill, man," Cute-but-awful guy said. He blew me a kiss and walked away.

I stood there on the dance floor breathing hard even though I wasn't moving. Mr. Darcy had rescued me. I knew I could have done it myself, but his method was way more effective and didn't involve bodily harm.

"Thank you," I told him over the music.

He shrugged like it was nothing. "May I have the next dance?"

He held out his hand, waiting for me to take it.

I hesitated. Not because I thought he would end up like Cute-but-awful guy, or because I didn't want to. I really *wanted* to dance with Mr. Darcy. I wanted to dance and then do so much more than dancing. And that's what scared me.

"You may," I replied, mimicking his formality before I

considered all the consequences. It was just a dance. What harm could a dance do?

The music changed to the next song. A steady, pounding bass beat thrummed across the dance floor like a heartbeat. My hips moved on their own to the tempo, dancing to the sultry music all on their own.

Mr. Darcy's hands went to my hips. They were strong and confident as he guided me in the motions of our dance. He knew exactly what he was doing as he put my body against his. I could feel the strength of his muscles under his jacket, and he moved with a natural grace.

The music throbbed, and I ached with it as Mr. Darcy danced with me. His hand glided down my side, teasing me with his touch while still being completely PG. The trace of his fingers left my skin tingling for more.

I wrapped my arms around the back of his neck, drawing the two of us in closer. There was nothing now but the two of us and the heavy, throbbing need of the music. His hips went slow with mine, keeping just enough distance without letting me forget where he was.

Every move was primal and sexual. Every cell in my body turned on, wanting to know what it would be like to feel this without clothes. My pulse pounded to the beat of the dance.

I bit my bottom lip, trying to keep myself grounded as I lost myself to him. Mr. Darcy was in complete control, and I was fine with that. He made every motion, every move, sexy as hell. It was sex on the dance floor and the hottest thing I'd ever experienced with my clothes on.

I looked up, my lip still between my teeth as I met his eyes.

Blue like the ocean, even in the dark of the club. They

captured me and held me there, stronger than any rope. I didn't want to leave the gaze of those eyes.

Emotions that I wasn't ready for flooded through me. I wanted him. I was incredibly attracted to him. I wanted to feel his skin under my fingers and see if he was this good a dancer in the bedroom. Heat flooded my core at the thought of the pleasure he was sure to give me. I was going to give into him.

Yet, somewhere, my brain came back. I knew he was an ass. He was a jerk just looking for his next lay. In that respect, he was no better than Cute-but-awful guy. He was just a better dancer.

I stumbled back, needing to figure out why my body was so attracted to him when my head knew better. I should never have danced with him. I should never have let myself feel the strength of the man under the suit.

My heel slipped, catching on the dance floor and my balance flew out the window. Yet, I didn't fall. Mr. Darcy rescued me, yet again. He pulled me into his body, holding me directly against him. His heart pounded with mine. I heated instantly, my skin crying out for his touch. If anything, the desire this time was almost unbearable.

I looked up again, finding those ocean eyes. They held a storm that I wanted to experience. I wanted to kiss him. I wanted to do so much more than just kiss him, but that seemed like a good starting point.

I licked my lips. He tipped his head, apparently thinking the same thing I was. I couldn't believe that I was about to do this, yet I wanted to so badly. My body was overriding my head and taking what it wanted.

I closed my eyes, letting myself go. This was what I wanted. A kiss to start.

The sharp chime of broken glass made us both look up before we connected.

I pulled away, the spell he'd woven over me broken. I couldn't believe what I was doing. I was going to kiss the man who bragged about me being an easy shag? It had to have been the champagne or the fact that he'd saved me. That was it. He'd saved me, and I wanted to kiss him because of that.

Sure. I could believe that.

I looked over at the broken glass to find my sister the cause of it.

She was up on the bar, dancing and knocking over drinks with every wobbly step. Two security guards were in the process of trying to get her down, but she was fighting them.

My heart sank. Why did she always have to go so far overboard to be noticed?

"Lydia!" I managed to get over to the bar just as the two guards set her on the ground. "What are you doing?"

She pulled her arms away from the guards and smoothed her hair. "What? How else am I supposed to get noticed? Have you seen how hot the people are here?"

Mr. Darcy pulled the guards to the side as I yanked my sister away from the broken glass.

"You can't dance on the bar," I told her.

"Why not? They are." She pointed to the professional dancers hired by the club dancing up on a different bar. One that wasn't covered in drinks.

"That's because they work here. You don't," I informed her. I looked over to see Mr. Darcy calmly speaking with the bouncers and pointing up toward the VIP area.

"It's fine, okay?" Lydia pushed me away. She was halfway back to the bar when the bouncers appeared in her path.

"Miss, you're going to have to leave," the bigger bouncer informed her. "We can't have you here being this disruptive."

"Do you know who I am?" Lydia asked, crossing her arms and throwing her chin up in the air. "I'm here with Charles Bingley. He owns this place. He owns you."

The bouncer lowered his head, so he was looking her straight in the eyes.

"That's the only reason you're still standing," he told her. "Anyone else would be out on their ass right now."

Lydia paled slightly, her face ghostly in the blue flashes of the dance lights. "Oh."

"Let the girl grab her things," Mr. Darcy told the bouncer. "She's on her way out. I'll make sure of it."

"Of course, Mr. Darcy," the bouncer replied, snapping up to attention. "Whatever you want."

Mr. Darcy motioned to the stairs, and Lydia did her haughtiest walk past the bouncers to get there. I half expected her to stick her tongue out as she passed them. I glared daggers at her the entire way up the stairs.

Despite Mr. Darcy's assurances, one of the bouncers followed behind us to make sure Lydia really was on her way out. To be honest, given the way Lydia was acting, I couldn't blame him.

Up at the table, Jane was giggling as she poured herself another glass of champagne. She looked more relaxed now, but that was only because she was drunk. Luckily, Jane was a terrific drunk. Alcohol simply made her giggly and silly.

"I have to take little Miss Dancing-on-tables home," I announced. "She got herself kicked out."

"What?" Jane's eyes went wide. She blinked twice before giving a stern glare to Lydia.

I pointed to Lydia's things and cleared my throat,

looking directly at my sister. Lydia rolled her eyes and stomped over to the far end of the table to retrieve them. While she did that, I knelt beside Jane.

"Are you going to be okay, Jane?" I asked, handing her a glass of water.

"I'm fine," she assured me, pushing away the water and reaching for more champagne. She was going to hurt in the morning if she kept this up.

"I'll make sure she gets home safely," Charles assured me. He grinned. "Her apartment is on the way home to mine."

I laughed. "Thank you, Charles. And I apologize for Lydia."

Charles waved his hand. "Don't worry about it. These things happen. She's still very young, and she knows what she wants."

"That's a nice way of putting it. Thank you for inviting us," I replied sincerely. "I had a great time."

I thought of my dance with Mr. Darcy and my body heated. I wondered what his skin felt like. I wondered if he would have tasted like the champagne. Now I'd never know. Which was probably for the best.

I glared at Lydia. "Time to go."

She rolled her eyes, and I tried to pretend that she had done me a favor. I was supposed to hate Mr. Darcy, so the last thing in the world I should be doing is wondering what his kisses would taste like. She was saving me from making a terrible mistake with him.

Still, I needed to thank him for helping keep the security guards away from Lydia. I looked around, but he was gone. All I saw was the back of his suit jacket and his phone up to his ear as he disappeared back toward the manager's office. He was working.

The bouncer stood with his arms crossed and tapping his foot for Lydia to make good on her promise to leave. Mr. Darcy had way too much faith in my ability to control my sister.

"Charles? Will you tell Mr. Darcy thank you for me? For helping with Lydia?" I asked. "He's off doing business again."

"Of course," Charles assured me. He had an arm around Jane's shoulder as she giggled and sipped on her drink. It looked like he'd managed to switch out her champagne for water at least.

With that, I grabbed Lydia's wrist and pulled her toward the stairs. She went willingly enough, but she did stop and wink at the bouncer for good measure. The girl was brave.

At the bottom of the stairs, I looked back up to see Mr. Darcy watching me. He simply looked at me. No wave, no nothing. Despite not moving an inch, he made my body respond. I wanted to sprint back up those stairs and beg for another dance. Lust and regret surged through me, tempting me to do something other than what I was doing.

Instead, I raised my hand to say goodbye and then hurried my sister out the door, telling myself it was the smart thing to do.

Chapter 8

$\mathcal{T}$he only good thing about leaving the club early was that the next day I didn't have a hangover. Unfortunately, neither did Lydia, so the experience taught her very little. Jane, on the other hand, was sick as a dog.

Charles had texted me during the night that she was going to sleep at his apartment. Jane didn't want me to worry about her, so she was having him text me. She was sick, and he didn't want to bother Lydia or me. He was going to make sure she was taken care of.

I had texted him back that I was happy to come up and get her, but he told me she was already settled and finally asleep. I wasn't about to interrupt their time together, even if Jane was sleeping through it.

I loved that he was so protective of her. They were a cute couple, and I knew he made Jane happy. The little bit of new love in the world made me smile. It was nice to know that there were still some good men out there, and even better to know that my best friend had found one of them.

I decided to go for a run through Central Park since it was my day off of work. Granted, it was much more of a "walk," but with the sunshine and crisp fall air, I didn't care. It felt good to be outside in the late autumn sunshine before winter arrived.

Besides, I needed something to do to keep my mind off of Mr. Darcy and our dance. All night, he was the only thing I dreamed about. And of course, we didn't stick to just dancing. I woke up in a sweat, desire seeping out of every pore with absolutely nothing to quench the fire inside of me.

Damn that man.

So, now I was out walking trying to clear my head and figure out what it all meant. Did he no longer hate me? Was this just a way to get that shag? Where in the world did he learn to dance like that? Would it be weird to ask Charles to take us to the club again? How could I still smell his cologne in my dreams?

"Lizzie!" Lydia yelled, breaking into my thoughts. She waved from the edge of the park, and I made my way over to her.

"I thought you were still sleeping," I said as I came to the sidewalk where she stood waiting for me.

"No, I had things to do," she replied. "I'm so glad I found you. I have amazing news!"

"You were cast as the lead in a blockbuster movie?" I asked with a smile.

"As good as! I'd like you to meet my new agent," Lydia announced. She turned to a handsome man standing beside her. "Elizabeth, I'd like you to meet George Wickham. He's got contacts all over New York *and* LA."

"Is that so?" I looked the man over, much more skeptical than my sister.

He was definitely attractive. He had Hollywood good looks with a strong jaw and broad shoulders. Soft blonde hair blew in the breeze, and his blue eyes sparkled in the sun. He wore a bright red jacket and stood with confidence.

"Please, call me Wickham. Everyone does," he said, holding out his hand. I didn't take it.

"And how much are your services costing my sister?" I asked, crossing my arms. I smiled, but it wasn't friendly.

"Not a dime," he assured me. "I don't make money unless she makes money. That's how it's supposed to work."

He handed me a business card with his name on it. He'd passed my first test.

"Feel free to check me out. I'm part of the Actor's Union. I'm the real deal," he explained. He gave me a megawatt smile. "I'm not a big name in the industry yet, but I have contacts that get roles. I'm here to get your sister parts, not take her money."

"The Actor's Union, huh?" I looked the card over in my hands. This felt a little less scammy than the last few "talent agents" Lydia had found. All the actor scams asked for money up front, and not a single one of them was affiliated with the Actor's Union. Lydia might have actually found a real agent.

"You're good to be concerned for your sister," he told me, brushing the blonde hair out of his face from the wind. "This industry is rough. There's a lot of scams and people who pray on dreams of getting into acting."

"We've met quite a few," I replied. I wasn't getting the same vibe from him that I usually did from her agents. I liked him and his friendly manner the more we spoke. "Many of the people we've talked to just want to take Lydia's money. They disappear after empty promises of breakout roles and ad campaigns."

"I am not one of those people," Wickham assured me.

"We're going to start small. I already have a contract that will be perfect for Lydia."

"What is it?" I asked. I couldn't help but be skeptical.

"It's how we met, actually," Lydia replied, tired of no longer being in the conversation. "He found me at the gym. He says I have a perfect face for print."

She grinned and did her best model face. I had to be honest, she was beautiful, but I wasn't about to get my hopes up. At least her ridiculously expensive gym membership might have paid off. She went to the most expensive gym in town, hoping for exactly this outcome.

"I was looking for attractive, fit young women for this campaign when I saw your sister on the treadmill," Wickham explained. "She's perfect for their image. I've already sent in her head-shots, and I'm hearing good things."

"I'm going to be famous, Lizzie!" Lydia jumped up and down with delight.

"Don't get too ahead of yourself," Wickham cautioned putting a calming hand on her shoulder. "We still have to get approved. But, it is a step in the right direction."

Lydia grinned at me. "I'm gonna be famous!" At least she didn't jump up and down this time.

I shook my head and smiled. This was the first time I actually had faith that Lydia had a shot. Wickham was a good fit. He wasn't filling her up with false dreams and wasn't just taking her money.

"And what's your cut if she gets this job?" I asked.

"The traditional ten percent," he replied. He gave me another disarming smile. "You're skeptical, and I like it. Seriously, check me out. I'm the real deal. I'd prefer it if we were working together to get your sister where she wants to go."

"I will," I said, pocketing his card. So far, I hadn't gotten any of the skeezy vibes I usually did off of Lydia's "agents." He hadn't asked for money, and he hadn't promised something he couldn't deliver. Plus, there was just something about him that was charming. He was certainly getting my mind off of Mr. Darcy, at least.

"Until then, can I interest you lovely ladies in a cup of coffee?" Wickham asked. He pointed to the opposite side road to the park, near the buildings. "There's a great coffee truck that stops just a couple of blocks over."

"I never say no to coffee," I replied. He just earned another point in my book.

"It's the best coffee this side of the Atlantic," he promised.

"Do you mean Lou's Coffee?" Lydia asked. The three of us walked in step along the sidewalk. Luckily, it was a quiet day in the park, so we were able to do so.

"Yes," Wickham said with a smile. "Do you know it?"

"Know it?" Lydia grinned. "I'm good friends with the owner."

"You seem to be good friends with all sorts of important people," Wickham told her. Lydia beamed. He obviously knew how to get on her good side.

"When you have talent, good looks, and an inheritance coming, it's easy," she replied with a laugh.

"An inheritance?" I asked her. She ignored me and hurriedly crossed the street, pulling Wickham along with her. I had to jog to keep up.

"So, keep going about the funny casting experience you were telling me about," Lydia said to Wickham, ignoring me and changing the subject of her supposed inheritance. She obviously didn't want Wickham to know she didn't have any money coming her way.

I sighed. I didn't want to confront her about this right

now. I was having a nice time, and I didn't want to ruin our walk by pointing out my sister's insane issues. I would just have to talk to her when we got home. As usual.

"Well, it was for a pudding commercial," Wickham replied. "And they needed people to look like they were experiencing the best pudding of their entire lives."

"I could do that," Lydia assured him.

"It came time for my client to show what she could do. The poor actress thought the casting director said 'old face' instead of 'O face' and I'm sure you can imagine what her audition looked like," Wickham said.

He squinted his eyes like he had poor vision, covered his teeth with his lips, and did the best impersonation of a blind, toothless old person I had ever seen. It was the exact opposite of what an "o-face" should have looked like.

I couldn't help but burst out into laughter.

"What did the casting director do?" I asked, covering my mouth as I tried to get control of myself. It didn't help that Wickham kept making the face as we walked.

"Well, he said it was the most original 'O-face' he'd ever seen and hired her on the spot," Wickham replied, putting his charming smile back on. "I still can't believe she got the job."

"And you say your clients are all that famous," I teased him. "Now, I know that one of those pudding girls is one of yours."

He chuckled. "You give me too much credit. She did all the hard work. All I did was set up the audition and make sure the contracts were in order. The real work is finding talent like Lydia."

Lydia fluffed her hair and grinned.

"Do you think they're going to use the 'old face' look in

the commercials?" I asked. "It would certainly make it more memorable."

"I think it would sell more pudding, so yes," Wickham replied, keeping a straight face. Then he made sure I was looking at him, and he made the "old face" again. I burst out laughing.

"Wickham, you're hilarious," I announced, reaching out to touch his arm.

"Elizabeth."

I looked up to see Mr. Darcy standing directly in front of me. He was dressed in a smart dark suit and acting for all the world like he owned the entire sidewalk. His blue eyes were only on me. My hand fell from Wickham, and my lungs forgot how to breathe for a moment as I had a vivid recall of our dance.

"Oh, hello," I stammered. My brain no longer seemed to know how to find words. "What are you doing here?"

"I had a meeting," he replied, his accent thick this morning. He motioned to one of the skyscrapers behind him. "And you?"

"I went for a run and ran into my sister and her new agent," I explained. I motioned toward Wickham. "Mr. Darcy, I'd like you to meet George Wickham."

Mr. Darcy's jaw tightened, and he barely made a nod of acknowledgment. The air temperature dropped ten degrees as the two men made eye contact.

I looked over at Wickham to see if the dislike was mutual, and found him looking sour. His full mouth was pinched and tight. There was some serious dislike and some sort of silent battle going on between the two of them that I didn't understand.

"If you'll excuse me, I have business to attend to," Mr. Darcy announced. He turned smartly on his heel and walked straight back into the skyscraper behind him. I stared after him, wondering what the heck had just happened.

"Oh, he's always like that," Lydia assured Wickham. "Lizzie actually hit him the first time she met him."

"I knew I liked you for a reason," Wickham said to me, a smile returning to his face as Mr. Darcy disappeared into the building. "There are many times I wish I would have hit him."

"I see the coffee truck," Lydia announced. "I'll order and get us a discount."

"Thank you, Lydia," Wickham said, beaming a handsome smile on her. "I'll take a number three, please."

Lydia preened in his attention. "No problem. I'll get you your usual, Liz." With one last grin for Wickham, she bounced off to order from the coffee truck.

"So, how do you and Mr. Darcy know one another?" I asked, watching my sister walk up and order.

"Unfortunately," Wickham replied. He offered me a sad smile. "We were step-siblings."

"Really?" I was shocked that these two men who clearly hated one another could be as close as siblings.

"My mother married his father when we were boys," he explained. "We grew up together."

"How come you don't have an accent?" I asked, trying not to sound too suspicious.

"My mother was American, and I spent most of my teenage years in America," he replied, luckily not sounding insulted at all. "I never really picked it up, but I do an amazing accent when drunk."

"I see," I said, nodding my head. "I'm guessing that you two aren't close then?"

"Oh, you noticed that?" He gave a self-deprecating

chuckle. "When William's father died, I was left a portion of the business in his will. But, William didn't like that, so he got his lawyers involved to call the changes invalid, and I never got any of it."

"Oh my gosh." I was shocked. "He did that?"

Wickham nodded slowly. "He did indeed."

I stood there, trying to take in this new information. Wickham should have been a billionaire board member of Oceanic Airlines, not a struggling talent agent. I had a hard time believing that Mr. Darcy could be so cruel, and yet... he *was* kind of a jerk.

"It was a long time ago," Wickham continued. "And I've made my peace with it. Luckily, even without the money, I still had friends in famous places. That's how I was able to become an agent."

"You've made lemonade out of lemons for sure," I told him. "I'm surprised you didn't walk right over and slug him."

Wickham shrugged. "The temptation was there, but it wouldn't accomplish anything." He put a hand on my shoulder and smiled at me with sweet eyes. "But, I don't want you to worry about me."

"If you say so," I told him. "Still, I'm sorry."

"Don't be," Wickham replied. "This wasn't my dream job, but I'm finding myself very good at. I'm discovering that I'm where I'm supposed to be. William will get his karma someday. I know it."

"I certainly hope so," I said. I was impressed by how well Wickham was handling this. If anything, it made me glad that he'd found Lydia. He would be good for her. If he could keep his temper around Mr. Darcy, he was already doing better than me.

"Here's your coffee," Lydia announced, holding out the

cups. "Lou says it's on the house in celebration of me getting an agent."

"Remind me to thank Lou," Wickham replied, gratefully taking his coffee.

I took a nice big sip of mine. Sweet vanilla with just a dash of cinnamon. Despite her flaws, Lydia knew my coffee preferences. She could be a good sister when she wanted to be.

"Now, tell Lizzie more about how you're going to make me famous," Lydia said, taking Wickham's arm as we began walking away from Mr. Darcy's building.

"I have big plans for you, Lydia," Wickham replied. "Big plans."

Chapter 9

"I can't believe that we get to go to the grand opening of the new hotel!" Lydia exclaimed, dancing around the kitchen in her little black dress.

"Considering that Jane is dating the owner, it's not that crazy. It's really sweet of Charles to invite us, though," I replied. I looked around, trying to find my shoes. "Lydia, did you borrow my black heels?"

"No. They're in the front closet," Lydia replied.

"Instead of in *my* closet where they belong?" I asked, putting my hands on my hips. She flashed me a big grin that told me she had totally borrowed them. I sighed.

"It's just too bad that Wickham couldn't get the night off," Lydia said with a sigh. "It would have been so nice to have an agent with me at the party. I can feel it in my bones that I'm going to meet a producer tonight."

"Remember, tonight is about Charles' new hotel, not finding a producer. Or an agent, or being discovered," Jane warned. "I don't want this night to end up all about you."

"Fine. You two act like I have no social skills at all," Lydia said, rolling her eyes dramatically. "Is the curling iron still on?"

I nodded, and she went to the bathroom to fix her already perfect hair. I went to the front closet to look for my black heels.

"I still can't believe what you told me about Wickham and Mr. Darcy," Jane whispered as I dug through a pile of shoes to find my heels. "It's probably a good thing that Wickham isn't coming tonight. It would just be awkward."

"I agree," I replied. I held up one shoe in triumph. I just needed to find the second.

"I have a hard time believing all of it, though," Jane continued. She reached in and pulled out my missing shoe. "There must be some sort of misunderstanding. Mr. Darcy doesn't seem that bad. And he's been so good to Charles."

"Oh, Jane," I said, taking the shoe from her. "You always believe the best in everyone. I don't think you're capable of thinking something bad about someone."

"And that's not a bad thing," Jane reminded me. She chewed on her cheek for a moment. "Did you tell Lydia about it?"

"She saw the whole meeting between the two of them," I told her. "I think she thinks the same thing about Mr. Darcy that I do."

Jane frowned. "I don't know. I'll ask Charles about it. Every story has two sides, and I want to make sure we know them both. It's only fair."

"It doesn't really matter," I told her, slipping on my shoes. They matched my sexy little black dress perfectly. "We already know he's an entitled, elitist ass."

"Be nice." Jane gave my shoulder a gentle push. "You're going to have to see him tonight."

I sighed. I wasn't looking forward to seeing Mr. Darcy.

Now that I knew the truth about him, I felt dirty even thinking about our dance.

"How are you and Charles doing, by the way?" I asked, changing the subject. I didn't want to think about Mr. Darcy unless I had to.

Jane's face melted into a happy smile. Her eyes went distant and wistful, and she let out a contented sigh.

"That good, huh?" I teased, giving her a grin.

She giggled. "I really like him," she said, looking down at her hands. She bit her lower lip and smiled. "I think he likes me, too."

"How could he not?" I asked her. "You're pretty amazing."

"I just wish we could have more private time together," she said, still looking at her hands. Her smile faded. "These openings and events are fun, but..." She sighed.

"But the crowds and photographers are too much for you," I finished, squeezing her shoulder. Jane nodded sadly.

"I really would prefer to just go to a movie. Or cook him dinner here," she said. "I don't feel like I belong up there in front of everyone."

I gave her a big hug. "You're doing great," I told her. "And you totally belong up there with him. You're gorgeous, and you belong."

She smiled weakly. "Thanks," she said with a shrug. "We should get going, or we're going to be late."

I nodded and grabbed our coats. I made sure Lydia turned off the curling iron (she hadn't) before we left, and together the three of us headed out of our building and down to a waiting limo. I was almost getting used to riding around in these things. It still felt luxurious to be chauffeured around the city this way, but I no longer felt like a newbie getting in and out of them.

Mr. Darcy and Charles weren't waiting for us in the limo this time. They were already at the grand opening of Charles' new hotel. There was a big party to show off the new building, and they were going to meet us there.

The drive was comfortable as we went to the far edge of the city to celebrate and see the new hotel. Lydia chattered happily as we drove, telling us how wonderful Wickham was and all the auditions she was going to go on.

About halfway there, Lydia pulled a flask out of her jacket and grinned. "Pre-game?"

"Yes, please," Jane said, reaching over and taking a big sip. She sighed as it went down. "I hate being out in public."

"Did you tell Charles?" Lydia asked. "Given the way he moons over you, he'd probably stop asking you to do this kind of thing."

"No." Jane held the flask in her hands and stared at it. She looked up at Lydia. "Because what if he decided not to invite me at all? It is his job, after all. I'd rather deal with the crowds and pictures than not be with him." She took another sip. "Besides, I think I'm getting better at it."

"You should just tell him," Lydia told her.

"Thanks, little sister," Jane replied, handing back the flask. I wasn't sure if she meant for the advice or the whiskey.

"Anytime, big sister," Lydia replied with a smile.

"My turn," I said, taking a swig. The whiskey burned on the way down with a beautiful warmth. I could feel it seep into my toes. If nothing else, this would make me more pleasant to Mr. Darcy if I couldn't manage to avoid him.

The limo stopped in front of a beautiful new hotel with a red carpet coming out the front door. Climbing out of the limo and stepping up onto that red carpet, I felt like I was important. It only got better as we walked right past everyone waiting to get in.

As soon as we stepped into the lobby, Charles came to greet us. Mr. Darcy was nowhere to be seen. Charles' smile was solely for Jane as cameras flashed all around us. She kissed his cheek and turned a bright shade of red as a camera flash clearly caught her in the act.

"I'm going to go make some new friends," Lydia announced. "Bye."

"Hey, behave yourself!" I called out to her. I didn't want another repeat of the gala. Or the club.

Please, please, please, let her not cause a scene this time, I prayed silently. I wasn't holding out much hope.

I found myself standing in the lobby by myself. Jane and Charles were off to the side, talking to another couple. It seemed like everyone in the room was paired off, and I was the lone man out. For a moment, I wished that Wickham had been able to come. He would have kept me company and kept me laughing through the night.

I smiled thinking of Wickham. I'd done some research on him and his talent agency. I'd found that he was a real agent with real clients. None of them were very famous yet, but he was slowly making a name for himself in the industry. I couldn't find much else on him, but I didn't find anything negative either. I was just glad he wasn't a scam.

I glanced around, finding only conversations already in progress. I decided I'd get a drink and then I could wander the new hotel. It was decorated beautifully with a large lobby leading into a comfortable lounge and bar. Everything sparkled.

I paused to notice one of the pieces of art hanging in the lounge on my way to the bar. It was the Gustave Loiseau painting from the fund-raising gala. I smiled to myself, knowing that Charles must have bought it and put it where he was sure Jane would see it. Having it displayed for everyone to see and enjoy would make her very happy.

I turned to walk away from the painting to get a drink and ran smack into Mr. Darcy's chest. He caught me as I bounced off of him, making sure that I didn't fall. He wore his trademark dark suit that fit him to perfection. His face was freshly shaven, and he smelled amazing because of course, he did. Memories of our dance and the passionate dreams that followed surged through me despite my best efforts to forget them.

"Oh, hello," I said once I regained my balance. I wasn't sure how to talk to him now that I knew the truth. I wanted to slap him again, but I knew that wasn't appropriate. I needed to pretend to be civil. For the sake of Charles and his opening, at the very least.

"Elizabeth," he greeted me. The way his accent curled on my name made me sound far fancier than I actually was. "Would you like to look around the hotel with me? I was hoping you would join me for a drink as we looked it over."

"Sure," I replied without thinking. My smile was brittle as I realized I just agreed to spend time with him. I didn't want to get a drink or anything else with him, but it was too late now.

"What would you like?" he asked, sounding like a gentleman, even if he wasn't one.

"Um, champagne is fine," I replied.

"I'll be right back. Stay here," he said, nodding his head and stepping away. I stared after him. Why in the world had I said I'd get a drink with him? I quickly came up with a plan to just disappear once he brought me my champagne. I'd say something polite, and go find Lydia. It wouldn't be that hard to get away. I didn't have to see the hotel with him.

"Are you okay?" Jane asked, coming up beside me. "You look like you might be sick."

"I might be," I replied. "I just agreed to a drink and a tour with Mr. Darcy. I can't believe I said yes."

"You're being too harsh," Jane scolded. "We haven't learned his side of the story."

"I don't need to have his side," I responded. She gave me a disappointed look, but I didn't take it back.

"Fine," she said with a sigh. "There's someone here I'd like you to meet."

I followed her to the lobby where a young woman was talking and laughing with Charles. They stood by a small standing table with a single rose centerpiece. It was exquisite and suited the hotel perfectly.

"Lizzie, I'd like to introduce you to Emma Woodhouse. She's a friend of Charles'," Jane said.

"It's a pleasure to meet you," I replied, holding out my hand. The young woman shook it and smiled.

"Excuse me," Charles said. "Jane, will you come take a photo with me?"

"Don't go anywhere. I need to talk to you," Jane whispered to me. "Just stay here."

I nodded. "Go take your picture. I won't go anywhere."

Jane forced a smile but went with Charles for the pictures she hated, leaving me with Emma.

"Jane tells me that you are a nurse?" Emma asked. "Is it anything like the TV shows?"

I smiled. "There aren't nearly as many good looking doctors. I can honestly say that I have never hooked up in a janitor's closet."

"Darn," she replied shaking her head. "TV falls short again."

I laughed. "I do love it though. It's a great job. Hard, but very rewarding."

"That's good to hear," she replied. She took a sip of her drink and motioned to the bar. "Did I see you speaking with William Darcy?"

"I was," I replied. "Do you know him?"

She shrugged. "A little. We spent some time together at a party in London once. He seemed like a decent person, but very busy with his business."

"That's a nice way of putting it," I said. "I'd say he's kind of a self-centered ass."

"Wow." She giggled. "You don't like him much," she noticed.

"He hurt a friend of mine over business," I replied. "I'm afraid that I'm not his biggest fan at the moment."

She nodded. "He does become rather cutthroat when it comes to his airline, but I think it's just because it's very important to him. When I met him, he was known for his charitable donations as much as his airline."

"Donations are just money, and he has plenty enough of that," I replied. "His behavior is inexcusable."

Emma tilted her head and looked at me thoughtfully. "It's a shame you don't like him," she said after a moment. "The two of you seem like a good match. I would have thought you two would hit it off."

I laughed. "No way. I have decided that Mr. Darcy and I are mortal enemies," I announced with a smile. "I think we have very different viewpoints on what is acceptable behavior in business."

"I can understand that," she replied with a nod. She waved to someone behind me. "Will you excuse me? I see an old friend."

"Of course," I told her. "It was a pleasure meeting you."

"And you. By the way, here he comes with some champagne for you." Emma smiled and touched my shoulder. "If you do have an epic battle with your mortal enemy, please don't mess up the lobby floor. Charles worked really hard to make it look nice."

I raised my hand like I was taking an oath. "I will not destroy the hotel," I promised her with a chuckle.

She grinned and picked her drink up off the tall table. She nodded a polite to hello to Mr. Darcy as she went to greet her friend. I wished Emma or Jane would come back and save me from having to talk to Mr. Darcy by myself.

"I didn't know what you preferred, so I brought my favorite," he said, handing me my drink.

I attempted a smile as I took a sip. At least it tasted good.

"It's good," I told him. "Thank you."

Silence fell between us, and I could hear a million other conversations in the lobby that sounded better than ours. I looked around for an escape, but there wasn't one. I was stuck having a drink. I thought about throwing the champagne in his face, but I didn't want to ruin Charles' party. I needed to play nice since I promised Jane I would.

"I'm afraid I'm not very discerning in my champagne tastes," I said after a moment. I needed to fill the silence, or I was going just to end up stewing and then reacting poorly. "This is good, though."

"It's Dom Perignon."

"It's very nice." I took another sip. I was going to need more if this was how the evening was going to go.

Mr. Darcy took another sip of his drink and nodded, leaving the silence between us to grow again.

"It's your turn to say something," I said after a moment. "That's how conversations work. I said something about the drink. You should say something about how the lobby is decorated or how well Charles did with this place. You should say something. Anything."

He looked at me with those mesmerizing blue eyes.

"Of course," he replied, lowering his glass. "What would you like to discuss?"

"You know, I'm not really sure," I said. I could hear the lyrics to a love song playing over the lobby sound system. "I guess we could just stand here in awkward silence. That seems to be working just fine."

Mr. Darcy took a sip of his drink, apparently unperturbed by my remarks. "Do you prefer the silence?" he asked. "Or I suppose we could talk politics?"

The idea of talking politics with Mr. Darcy made me wince. "I have a feeling that talking politics would leave us screaming obscenities at one another."

"I think we're probably more alike than you think," he replied, a knowing smirk crossing his face. I did my best to ignore the impulse to knock it off his smug head.

"What about your business?" I offered. "That seems to be the only thing that interests you."

A hint of irritation crossed his features. "Why do you say that?"

"It's all you seem to do," I replied, feeling self-satisfied in my small victory against him. I'd gotten under his skin with that comment. "You're always on the phone. It seems like you never stop working."

He took a slow sip of champagne. I watched his Adam's apple bob as he swallowed. He smiled at me.

"How are your patients in the CICU?" he asked. He was obviously avoiding talking about business just to prove me wrong.

I was not expecting that, but it was a nice deflection. Fine. I could play that game.

"They're doing well," I replied. "I actually just discharged one yesterday. He had a triple bypass and was a wonderful man with a kind family."

"I'm glad to hear it," Mr. Darcy said, almost managing to sound sincere.

I decided it was time to play hardball. I set my drink down on the high table.

"In fact, he says his daughter is an actress and would be happy to give Lydia some pointers," I continued. "He actually congratulated my sister on acquiring an agent so early in her career."

"Wickham is lucky to have such skill acquiring talent," Mr. Darcy replied diplomatically. He lowered his glass, and his eyes hardened. "If he can give her any success, I'll be incredibly impressed."

"As long as you don't sabotage him, he should be fine," I retorted.

His nostrils flared, and he set his drink down on the table harder than necessary. I'd finally riled him, and it felt good. My heartbeat sped, and I moved closer.

"I do not sabotage. I do not cheat. I do not make false promises that I can't keep," he said, enunciating every word. His hand gripped the glass hard enough I was afraid he might break it.

I wasn't about to back down, though. I wanted this out in the open. I wasn't going just to let this be. I wanted answers. I wanted him to be accountable for his actions.

"And you say that Wickham does? You say he sabotages and cheats?"

"That is for you to determine," Mr. Darcy replied. He narrowed his eyes at me. "I will not speak poorly of him. Why are you pressing this?"

"Because I want to know why," I replied, taking a step

toward him. I wanted to get under his skin and annoy him as much as he annoyed me. I wanted him to think of me the way I did him: often and without meaning to.

"I'll tell you anything you want to know," he said, his voice low and dangerous. He was close to me now. I didn't remember taking quite this many steps into him, but I was close enough now to smell his cologne. I could see the blues and grays of his eyes and the small spot he missed shaving near his earlobe.

How did he infuriate me so easily? Why did being near him cause my heart to go crazy and my ability to think disappear? I glared up at him, riled and looking for a fight. I wanted to get a reaction out of him. I wanted him to react to me.

I wanted to knock him down and kiss him, and I wasn't sure it was in that order. The space at the arch of my legs ached for something only he could give me. I hated him, yet my body wanted his touch. Lust surged through me in hot waves.

I hated that I wanted him, but that only made me want him more.

How did he get under my skin and turn me on?

Without thinking, without my brain's permission, my body leaned forward and kissed him.

And oh, God, did it feel good.

Every part of my body sang with need and kissing him made it better and worse at the same time. He threaded his hand behind my head and into my hair, kissing me back.

And the man could kiss. His lips were soft, yet demanding. He tasted better than he had in any of my dreams. Sweet, yet rich with hints of champagne.

Before I knew what I was doing, I wrapped my arms around his neck, not letting him go. I needed his kisses, his touch, and so much more. I needed him more than I needed to breathe. I hated him and needed him in equal parts.

What in the world had he done to me? I went from hating him to wanting to screw him in the space of a single kiss.

"We should go someplace less public." He broke the kiss just long enough to whisper the words, and even then that was too long.

I nodded, hating that he pulled away from me. My body ached to feel him against me, and even though I knew I would get more, I hated that I didn't have him that instant.

He grabbed my hand. With my lips still tingling from Mr. Darcy's kiss, he pulled me away from the crowd.

Chapter 10

$\mathcal{M}$r. Darcy held my hand in his as he hurried up the stairs. I could barely keep up on my heels as we went, but there was no way I was letting go of him. Not now. Not with this heat and need coursing through my veins.

Anger and fury had transformed into need and lust.

The second floor of the hotel was deserted. Everyone was downstairs and in the ballrooms enjoying the festivities, so no one was up here. Mr. Darcy looked up and down the length of an empty hallway before pressing me up against the wall and kissing me.

The kiss exploded into me as a hot, intense tangle of tongues and teeth. Everything was raw desire as my mouth found his. One hand gripped my hip as the other tangled in my hair, pulling me into him. I wanted more than this, but it was a good start.

My hands slid into his jacket and started undoing the buttons on his shirt. I could feel the muscle and tension beneath my fingers. I fumbled with the tiny buttons, unable to focus with the onslaught of all the emotions: hunger, desire, need, and something that made my knees tremble with his touch.

"More," I whispered, my voice coming out in gasps. "Please, more."

He groaned, the sound vibrating through my world. He lowered his head so that his breath warmed my neck. Need ached through my core. My anger had turned to lust, but it was still all-consuming and overpowering. All the intensity from the lobby was now here with just the two of us alone in this hallway.

He took a step back and pushed on one of the doors to a room. It didn't budge. He tried the next, but again it didn't move. I knew that if we stopped and we went back downstairs and got a key, we would lose this momentum. We would stop and think about what we were doing and think better of it.

Right now my body was in control. My head was lost to the overwhelming desire and need pumping through me. I didn't want to stop. I knew that this was probably a mistake. We were both angry, and it was translating into something more.

I didn't say a word. I just kept trying doors, waiting for one to open up. I was off balance, and my body was in control. I needed Mr. Darcy. I knew it had to be him. He was the reason I was off balance and doing this crazy thing. He was the one under my skin and pushing all my buttons. He was the only man I'd ever met that made me feel this way.

He did something to me that I didn't understand, but I wanted more of it.

"Here," he called to me, pushing the door to a room open. I followed him without hesitation.

Inside, he pressed me against the wall again, the door swinging past me and clicking shut. I reached for it, searching for a lock, but couldn't find one. It wasn't a lock-able door. Someone could walk in on us.

But, I didn't care. All I cared about was wrapping my legs around this man and releasing the tension building inside of me. I was out of control now. There was no turning back. He kissed me, his hands searching my body and I moaned.

I kissed his throat, flicking my tongue against the sensi-tive skin there. He tasted amazing, and the groan he let out went straight to my loins. He slid his hands down to cup my ass in his palms, pulling me into him as he pushed me into the wall.

"Elizabeth." I loved the way my name sounded on his low, gravelly voice. I writhed with smug satisfaction, knowing I was having the same effect on him as he was on me. Out of control lust.

I lifted my head, and his mouth came down on mine again. His hips pressed into mine and I could feel him growing hard. I heated just knowing that I had this effect on him.

"Do you want this?" he asked, those blue eyes holding me still. I was still pinned to the wall, my hands on his chest and panting with desire.

Did I want this? Oh, hell yes I did.

I leaned forward and nipped at his bottom lip, feeling feminine and in control.

"Yes," I whispered. I undid the button on his shirt, followed by another. I looked up, rocking my hips into his. "I do."

The words came out steady and sure. I did want this. I wanted this more than anything I could ever think of. Maybe I just hated him because he turned me on and made me lose control of myself. Maybe I didn't hate him at all, and the energy between us was misplaced lust.

Either way, I wanted this. I wanted more.

You do this, and you'll fall for him, a small voice said in my head. I looked up into those blue eyes and realized I could deal with that. Jane would be proud of me for giving him a chance.

His eyes stayed steady on mine. He swallowed hard before kissing me again. It started gentle, but then I moaned, and he lost control for a moment. His hands tightened on my hips, and his kiss devoured me.

I undid the rest of his buttons, and he shrugged off his jacket, followed by the dress shirt. He barely broke the kiss to take off his undershirt and toss it to the ground. The man worked out. He was all pecs and abs under his suit, and my mouth went dry.

How was I this lucky?

He kissed me again, this time pulling me away from the wall with small steps and further into the room. It appeared to be some sort of conference room with a large table in the center. There weren't any chairs yet since the hotel was so new. The windows had shades pulled lows but the lights of the city still shined through them.

I reached for the zipper of my dress, stretching and straining to reach it. I didn't care that I probably looked the opposite of sexy. I wanted it off.

"Let me," he said softly, gently pushing on my shoulder to turn me around.

I shivered as his hand caressed the bare skin of my shoulders as he found the zipper. I put my hands on the conference table just to keep myself steady. His fingers were careful and slow as he tugged on the zipper and exposed my back to him.

The little black dress puddled on the ground around my heels and my breath caught. It was cold in the room without the dress, and my nipples hardened even further. I hadn't worn a bra with the dress, all I had on was a teeny-tiny lace thong and my heels.

I bit my lower lip, unsure if I wanted to turn around or not. He was a billionaire who had been with supermodels. I was happy with my body, but to be honest, I liked my cookies. I wasn't supermodel status.

All my thoughts scattered when Mr. Darcy pressed himself to my back. He still had on his dress pants, but his excitement was evident. His bare chest was hot against the skin of my back, and I gasped. He slid his hands up the front of my thighs, nudging them apart with his knee.

I gasped with raw desire when he ran a fingertip along the lace edge of my panties. I shivered with want as he played with the soft fabric, cupping his hand over the flimsy material. His other hand slid across the skin of my stomach and up to a breast.

His fingers were gentle yet insistent as he played with the fabric. He teased me through it, his hips pinning me in place to the table as he worked his magic. My back arched into him, and he used his mouth on my shoulders and throat.

"Please," I moaned, hanging on the edge of pure pleasure. I just needed a little bit more of a push.

"Tell me what you want," he whispered. His voice caressed me in the dark of the room.

"Touch me. Take me."

He nipped at the soft spot where my shoulder met my neck just as he slid his fingers under the fabric and touched me directly.

The electricity of skin to skin was nearly enough to do me in, but he pulled back before I could find completion. I whimpered He kissed my shoulder and spun me around.

"I want to watch you," he told me, a devilish grin crossing his face. He looked me up and down, his pupils going wide. "Damn, you're beautiful."

The authenticity of the compliment made me freeze for a moment, and he took advantage of it. He lowered his head to a bare breast as his hand went back to the small triangle of lace and pushed it to the side. His thumb made tiny circles as a finger slid in deep.

He moved in slow stroking motions, working his thumb and his fingers in perfect harmony with my body. Every nerve ending started to tingle as he stoked the fire deep in my belly with his touch. His tongue worked my nipple, teasing it as he worked.

One hand threaded through his dark hair, holding him in place to me as my breath came hard and fast. The room spun until all that was left was Mr. Darcy and the pleasure he gave me. The pleasure I craved.

Everything hummed and throbbed as I crumpled into him. Exquisite pleasure ripped through my body, pouring out of every nerve as I froze and writhed at the same time. I would have fallen into a helpless puddle of vibrating pleasure on the floor if he hadn't held onto my hips.

"Damn," I squeaked, my voice unsure of how to work after such an intense orgasm.

He grinned, his smile cocky as hell and pupils wide with enjoyment. He rubbed his thumb in a tighter circle making me whimper with the pleasure of his touch.

But now I wanted more.

I reached down and caressed the hard length of him through his pants. He jerked into my touch, moaning with pleasure. I felt like the queen of sex knowing I had this effect on him. He looked up at me with those blue eyes, and I knew that it was true.

Lust, desire, want- they all burned there in blue fire. My breath caught at the intensity of it. He wanted me in a way I'd never seen anyone want me. It was pure and unbridled. My body lit to his touch, eager to play with that fire.

"More," I whispered again. "More, please."

He smiled a predatory grin that made my knees go weak as he put his hands on my hips and lifted me up onto the table. It was cold on my bare skin, the tiny string of thong not providing any protection. I gasped but didn't pull away. If anything, I simply spread my legs.

I reached for his belt and tugged it free while he undid the button and zipper, kicking his pants to the side. He was a boxer-briefs man, and they did him credit. I reached for the waistband, wanting to see what was underneath causing his poor underpants to nearly explode.

That's when the doorknob twisted.

My eyes went wide, and my hands went to cover my naked breasts, but if someone walked in, there was no place for me to hide.

Mr. Darcy moved like a cat, his hand on the back of the door holding it in place. The handle moved up and down, and I held my breath.

"Try another room. This one's locked," a male voice said. "There's got to be one around here."

A female voice giggled. It was just another couple looking for a room in the new hotel.

Mr. Darcy held the door still. The voices faded, but he kept his hand on the door until he was sure they were gone. I didn't know how much longer we would have before we would be interrupted again. Without a lock on the door, there was a very good chance that we could be caught.

At this moment, I didn't care. Not with him standing there looking hotter than sin and me ready to drown in him.

If there was an upside to almost getting caught, it was the fact that he now had to walk back toward me. The man was all long, lean lines that my fingers itched to touch. I wanted to lick the paths leading to a V above his legs. It was incredibly lick-able.

I grinned as he pulled off his underwear before casually crossing the room. He was the embodiment of cockiness and confidence, and my body shivered with anticipation. He stopped at his pants, pulled a condom from his pocket, and carefully slid it on.

He took two measured strides before he was back between my legs.

I spread my legs wider, tempting him into me. He waited, his hard parts pressed deliciously up against my soft ones, teasing me with what came next. One hand moved the tiny bit of fabric to the side, and there was nothing left to stop him. His finger traced my cheek in a gentle caress. It was so much sweeter than I expected and my throat tightened.

Was this more than just sex? It suddenly felt like it could be.

He kissed me, and I forgot everything else. Everything except him and the promise of wrapping myself around him vanished. My body took over, and I arched my hips, drawing him into me. His hand tightened on my hips, and the low, male noise nearly sent me spiraling into orgasm.

It started slow, with just a gentle rocking of his hips. Every slow inch, by inch, by aching inch until he filled me to the point of almost pain. Still, I wanted more. I needed it over and over again. He retreated, and I whimpered until he moved forward and filled me once again.

I watched as he tucked his head into my shoulder, watching himself fill me again and again. I loved watching it too. I reveled watching him take me, feeling the pleasure of him overwhelm me yet again.

I'd never had anything like this. I'd never ached to have someone go deeper than before or to crave just another inch of skin to press into mine. I'd never felt this hot and full of intense need. I craved him like I craved oxygen and he delivered.

Desperation forced me to buck my hips, wanting more than this slow and sensual torture. The pleasure building deep in my core needed a release, and the slow burn wasn't going to do it for me.

"Harder," I whispered, looking into his eyes. The blue fire flared, and he pressed deep.

His hands gripped my hips, my legs wrapped around his ass and my hands pulled him into me. The weight of his muscled chest and abs pressed into me. His muscles strained with the effort as he tried to maintain control.

"Elizabeth," he groaned, struggling to keep himself from losing himself. It was my name that undid me. The sheer urgency and desire in every syllable skyrocketed me into coming so hard I couldn't tell up from down. All I knew was that he came with me.

He buried his face in the crook of my neck, his body shaking with mine in the ultimate pleasure. I couldn't let go. All of the passion, all of the fight, all of the anger had turned into sheer pleasure that rocked through both our bodies.

We both were breathing hard. I knew that at any moment someone might walk through that door and find us. I didn't want to move. I didn't want this perfect moment to end. We were one, and it felt more right than anything ever had.

"Elizabeth," he whispered, his voice ragged and raw. It made me shiver and start to heat all over again.

I whimpered, keeping him pulled into me. I wanted his skin against me. I wanted this all over again and again.

From across the room, his pants started to vibrate and hum.

"Don't go," I whispered, locking my arms around him.

"I have to at least check it," he replied, kissing my temple. I sighed as he stroked my hair back and kissed my forehead.

Reluctantly, I released him. The loss of his touch was a physical pain. It was cold and sharp as I waited for him to look at his phone. I grinned as I thought of us getting a room. It didn't even have to be a nice room. Just someplace with a bed. Oh, the things I wanted to do with him in a bed.

The table was good, but a bed would be even better.

Maybe the shower, too.

I looked over to see him putting his pants on as he held the phone up to his ear. I frowned but didn't say anything. Maybe it was just a quick phone call. He did have a business to run. A quick phone call, followed by a trip to a real room would be fine.

"This is Darcy," he said, his voice calm and in control. It was the same and yet so different than the voice that had just gasped my name.

He was nearly fully dressed again. His shirt was still unbuttoned, but other than his shoes and jacket, he was dressed. I still sat practically naked on the table.

He paused at whatever the other person on the other line said. He held still for a moment before looking at me.

"Is it absolutely necessary?" he asked. His face went hard at the answer. "One minute."

He kissed my forehead and then walked out of the room.

I watched the door swing shut and click softly behind him. His voice disappeared down the hallway.

Still, I waited. I waited until I was cold and shivering. I stood up, the heat from before no longer there. Now there was just emptiness.

I struggled to put my dress back on, fighting with the zipper until I had it most of the way back up. I kept hoping that every footstep outside in the hall was him, but they always kept going.

I looked around the room once I was dressed again. It seemed sad instead of romantic now. The shades were cheap and the missing chairs obvious.

My throat tightened as I realized he wasn't coming back.

He was gone without saying a word.

My chest clenched and I fought back the tears. I was better than this. I was so much more than this. Was the connection, the intensity of it, just in my head?

I sniffled. I had nothing to show that there was anything between us.

I was nothing more than an easy shag. One I did for bragging rights.

I picked up my phone and messaged Jane that I didn't feel well and was heading home. The party was over.

Chapter 11

"*I* feel stupid, oh so stupid, it's amaaazing how stupid I FEEEEL," I sang softly to myself. No one on the subway even looked at me strangely. People singing on the subway wasn't considered weird in New York City. I half expected someone to throw me a dollar.

I pressed my forehead into the cool glass of the window and watched the dark brick walls of the subway pass by. I felt so stupid.

Why in the world did I sleep with him?

I couldn't wrap my head around it. I could understand that he was the most attractive man I knew. I could see how that might make me do something I now regretted. I wanted to pretend that I'd had some whiskey and some champagne, so I probably wasn't in full control of my faculties. I knew that was a lie.

I'd known exactly what I'd been doing when I slept with him.

I'd wanted it.

And now I was paying for my stupidity.

I checked my phone again, but there wasn't a single

message from him. He'd slept with me, walked out on me, and then didn't even have the decency to call me the next day.

He just didn't want to talk to me. He'd gotten what he wanted. A *shag*.

I was an idiot, and he was a total ass.

I sighed and hummed my stupid song to myself again. I'd been singing it all day at work. I only had one patient, which meant that I had way too much time to sit and think. I kept hoping that a difficult patient would arrive, just so I could concentrate on something else, but everyone stayed miraculously heart-attack free.

Great for patients, bad for me.

My phone stayed silent in my hand, just like it had all day.

It wasn't like it would be hard to get my number. He was a billionaire, and his best friend lived in the same building and was dating my roommate. Hell, he could have just sent Charles down to say something.

I sighed and knew that was stupid too. What in the world would he have Charles say?

"Hey, thanks for shagging my friend." Or perhaps, "He wants to marry you and have your babies, but he had something really important come up last night. Sorry. All the apologies."

Any way that I looked at what happened last night, I was an idiot. I knew he was terrible, although sexy as hell. I should never have gone upstairs with him. I should have stayed away.

I got off at my station and stomped my way home. It was dark now, but in New York City, it was never really dark. The lights were everywhere in the city.

I grumbled the whole way up the elevator to my apartment. I wanted to talk to Jane. I wanted her to tell me that I had simply given into my passions and that I wasn't a complete moron. I wanted her to tell me that he was a terrible human being and that she would have Charles beat him up for me.

I needed her calm and sweet approach to this.

I threw open the door, ready to tell her what had happened the night before. I hadn't seen her since I had to go to work early and had beaten her home last night.

I found her sitting on the couch, staring at the "Are you still watching?" screen on the TV. A half a container of ice cream sat melting on the couch next to her. Jane's face was covered in tear stains.

"Jane, what's wrong?" I asked, forgetting my problems, dropping my purse, and running to her side.

Whatever kind of trance she was in broke as soon as she saw me and she burst into tears. Giant sobs racked her body.

"He's gone," she cried. I had a hard time understanding her.

"What?" I moved the ice cream off the couch and opened my arms to hold her.

"He's gone," she told me, putting her head on my shoulder and letting me hold her as she cried. "Charles is gone."

"What do you mean Charles is gone?" I asked, rubbing her back. "Why would he leave?"

Jane shrugged. "He says he has to build a hotel in New Jersey and that we shouldn't be a couple while he's gone." She took in a deep, shaky breath, trying to compose herself but failing.

"I don't understand," I said. "He was supposed to be in New York all winter for the opening of his new buildings. Did that change?"

"No, he's still here. He lied. I don't know why, but he lied to me. He just doesn't want me."

"Jane, I'm sure that's not true," I replied. I thought of the goofy happy look on his face whenever he saw her. "He loves you. He must have something to do in New Jersey."

"No, he doesn't." Jane sniffled and handed me the newspaper. "He just wanted an excuse to break up with me. He said we're not a couple anymore."

I looked at the article she was pointing to as a fresh wave of tears overtook her. It was definitely Charles, and he was definitely in New York City. The worst part was that there was a beautiful blonde woman hanging off his arm and looking up at him like he was the light of her life.

The caption under the picture said *New love interest? You decide!*

My heart broke for Jane. My own problems seemed so much smaller right now.

"I'm so sorry," I whispered, hugging her close to me. Poor Jane simply cried, her heart completely broken.

I looked over at the article. I could hardly believe it. The article continued that Charles Bingley had recently taken up a new residence in Manhattan. I shook my head. Manhattan was not New Jersey.

I had thought the two of them were happy. I had thought they were the relationship that would make it. I was wrong.

Yet another thing I was wrong about.

"You know what?" I said, an idea coming into my head. "Tomorrow is my day off. I'm taking you out for some shopping. We're having a girl's day out."

"A girl's day out?" Jane wiped at her cheek. Her beautiful face was splotchy and so sad.

"Yup." I nodded, liking my plan more and more. "Just the two of us. We'll talk smack about men and get our nails done. We'll eat carb filled, fatty, clog-our-arteries-bad-for-us food and try on beautiful dresses just for fun."

"I don't know, Lizzie." She sniffled. "It hurts so much. I loved him."

I hugged her tighter. "I know. And I don't know what he's thinking. He's an idiot for letting you go."

She sniffled and cried into my shoulder.

"You know what, I'm going to go beat him up," I announced. "Do you have a baseball bat I can borrow?"

"No, Lizzie, don't do that."

"No? I guess it would damage your baseball bat, and that's not worth it," I agreed. Jane chuckled a little, and it made my heart ache for her that much more. "Please let me try and cheer you up a little?"

"We can go out tomorrow," she agreed. "I spent all day home today. I should find a way to get over him."

"Good," I told her, trying to keep my voice light. "Now, let's put you to bed. Some sleep will do you good."

Jane didn't protest. She didn't object when I gave her some sleeping medicine and sent her to bed. She went quietly into her room and turned out the light without a fight. Which only made my heart ache for her even more.

Love didn't exist, I decided. It was all fake. It was all just a lie to get us into bed and break our hearts.

I took Jane's spot on the couch and finished her ice cream because I needed the comfort.

Chapter 12

"That one makes your butt look amazing," I said to Jane, checking out her form in the mirror. "Seriously, your booty is out of this world in that dress."

Jane laughed and turned so she could see herself better in the mirror of the dressing room.

"I do have a pretty fabulous ass," she admitted with a giggle.

"That's the spirit," I said with a grin. "You should try on the pink one next."

"You mean the one with the slit down to here?" She pointed to her bellybutton. "No way."

I raised my eyebrows at her. "You know you want to."

She rolled her eyes. "I'd never actually wear it."

"And you'd wear this one?" I pointed to her current dress. It was bright red satin and hugged every inch of her so tightly that only her skin color was left to the imagination.

"Good point," she conceded. She picked up the pink dress and headed toward the changing room. She paused at the door, turning to look back at me. "Thank you for this, Lizzie. I'm having fun."

"Good. My evil plan is working," I teased, dry washing my hands like an evil mastermind. It made Jane laugh as she went to change.

I sat in the plush viewing area of an upscale dress store and sipped on a glass of champagne. Everything here was way out of our budget, but they didn't know that. We had stepped in to look at the prices and see if anything was on sale when the attendant recognized Jane from her pictures in the paper.

Suddenly, we were set up in a private dressing area with champagne flutes. We decided to go with it and try on some of the more outlandish dresses. If nothing else, it was making Jane laugh.

"Holy mackerel," I said as Jane stepped out. She looked like a model in a fashion magazine. "Wow."

"There is no way I would ever wear this in public," she announced, her hands hovering over the major slit running down the front of the dress. It showed off her cleavage and every curve of her body.

"You look hot," I told her. "And you couldn't wear that in public because the first man that saw you would lose his mind."

"Lose his mind, huh?" She looked over in the mirror. "Maybe I should wear it to a hotel opening."

"We agreed we aren't talking about him," I reminded her. "No men today. Just girl fun."

She sighed. "Sorry."

"Jane, repeat after me: No, you can't have this. I'm far too good for you," I said in my most dramatic voice.

She giggled. "I'm not saying that."

"Do it," I pushed.

"No, you can't have this," she said flatly. She giggled and finished with a little flair. "I'm far too good for you."

"Not bad," I said with an appreciative nod. "I would nominate you for an Academy Award, but you'd probably win, and you know how Lydia would feel if you got an Academy Award before her."

"Win or lose, Lydia would kill me either way," she replied with a laugh.

I looked down at my watch. "Shoot, we're going to be late for our reservation."

"I'll go change," she said, taking one last look at herself in the mirror.

"I'm far too good for you," I repeated, using even more drama this time.

Jane stuck out her tongue at me and went to change.

I checked my phone for an update from Lydia while Jane was busy. Lydia was supposed to be doing some sort of photo-shoot work today. It was at a car dealership outside of town, but it sounded like honest work. She had already sent me two pictures of her in a bikini on an expensive looking car. It wasn't my idea of work, but as long as Lydia was happy and getting paid, I didn't object.

Jane came out of the changing room, and we snuck out of the store before the salesperson could pressure us to buy anything. I was tempted to pick up the pink dress as a surprise, but it was way more than I could afford on a whim. Still, it had been fun to play dress-up.

"Where are we going for lunch?" Jane asked as we walked along some shops. "I'm starving."

"Here," I told her as we came around the corner of the shopping center. I pointed to the fancy upscale restaurant before us.

Jane's mouth hung open. She shook her head. "Lizzie, we can't afford that."

The restaurant was super fancy. It was the type of place that I suspected Mr. Darcy and his friends liked to visit as they made fun of the lower classes.

"You're not supposed to," I told her. "I'm buying it as a treat to make you feel better."

"Lizzie, you can't afford that," Jane amended.

"We're just going to get an appetizer and drinks," I replied. "I have plans to pick up a pizza on the way home. But, I did want you to have something special."

"Now that, I can get behind," Jane said with a laugh. "I've always wanted to try this place."

"Why do you think I brought you here?" I gave her a gentle shoulder bump. "I'm supposed to make you feel better. I thought this might help."

Jane smiled at me. "You're a good friend."

"Sister," I replied. "You know we're sisters."

Jane grinned and nodded. "Damn straight."

Even though we weren't all biological sisters, Jane was as much a sister as Lydia and I were. We'd grown up together and then practically adopted Jane when her parents died. She was a part of my family, and I would protect her and treat her like one. She certainly treated Lydia and me like her sisters.

Together we walked into the fancy restaurant with smiles on our faces.

"Hello, I have a reservation for Bennet," I informed the hostess.

She scanned the book in front of her. Her finger paused on an entry, and her smile flickered for a moment before she looked up.

"I'm so sorry, but we don't have your reservation on file," she replied.

"We can just go-" Jane started to say, but I put my hand on her shoulder.

"You don't have it?" I repeated. "You're sure? I made it this morning."

"I'm afraid it's not in here." She blinked rapidly, betraying the lie. "But, I can seat you at the bar."

"That will work," I said with a sigh. It wasn't like we were eating an actual meal here, anyway. The bar would be fine.

"I'm so terribly sorry for the change," she said with a practiced smile as she led us to a beautiful mahogany bar. Since it was past lunch, we had our choice of seats. Jane chose a small bar table near the window so we could look out over the city.

"I can't believe they lost our reservation," Jane remarked, picking up a drink menu.

"They didn't," I replied. "They gave our table away. I saw her pause where my reservation should have been. Someone more important stole our table."

"No, I'm sure that's not it," Jane said shaking her head. "Mistakes like this happen all the time."

"Jane, you are too forgiving," I told her with a smile. "Let me buy you a drink."

"A martini," she said with a grin. She pointed to the menu. "This one sounds sufficiently fancy."

"Coming right up," I said, standing up. I walked over to the bar and ordered two martinis. While the bartender worked, I flipped through a menu for our appetizer options. The lobster ravioli with truffle butter sounded terrific.

The bartender handed me the two drinks and I walked carefully back toward our table. I was less than a step away when I heard him.

"Elizabeth?"

I knew that voice. It made my blood heat and my stomach drop. I froze in mid-step, trying to decide what reaction I wanted to follow.

I wanted to turn and throw both drinks in his face, but they were expensive and I didn't want to waste good vodka on him.

"Mr. Darcy! What a pleasant surprise," Jane greeted him, a smile filling her face. She didn't see my wide eyes and the subtle head shake I was trying to send her. Given her state last night, I hadn't told her about what happened between Mr. Darcy and me yet. As far as she knew, everything was sunshine and roses between us. Or at least as much as there ever had been.

"Indeed," Mr. Darcy replied. "Are you two waiting for a table?"

"Nope," I quickly replied. I turned and put on my best bitchy smile. "We're actually just finishing."

An older man in a smart blue suit came up and tapped Mr. Darcy on the shoulder. "William, our table is ready."

"Excellent," Mr. Darcy replied. "Fritz, I'd like to introduce you to Elizabeth and Jane.

Fritz's gray eyebrows raised and he smiled. "It's a pleasure to meet you both," he replied warmly. "Would you care to join us? They gave us a table for four."

I looked at Jane, giving her my best "no way in hell" look.

"We'd love to," Jane replied, clearly not understanding my look.

We were going to have to work on her reading my signals better.

Jane stood from the bar table and took her drink from me. I tried to grab her shoulder, to make her stop so that we could leave. I didn't want to spend a moment more with Mr.

Darcy. I missed her shoulder though and only succeeded in spilling some of my drink on my hand.

I did the only thing I could do. I put on what I hoped would pass for a pleasant smile and followed behind her.

"This is a beautiful restaurant," Jane remarked as we walked through the room. Every table was full of dining guests all eating fabulous looking food. Fritz guided the four of us to the only open table.

"It's my favorite," Fritz replied to Jane. "I make poor William come here every time I'm in town. It was a last minute visit today, and he still found a way to get us a table."

My teeth ground together. Mr. Darcy took my table. It had been my reservation that he stole. Yet one more reason to hate the bastard.

"Where are you visiting from?" Jane asked as Fritz held out a chair for her. Mr. Darcy did the same for me and I did my best to ignore him.

"I manage William's West Coast division," Fritz replied. "I think I've been in the company almost as long as he has."

"If we're interrupting a business meeting, we can go," I offered, already rising to my feet. "It's really not a problem."

"Please stay." Mr. Darcy's voice was quiet, yet sure. He looked at me with those blue eyes and I was once again powerless to say no to him. Damn him.

"Yes, please stay," Fritz chimed in. "We already finished talking business."

I slowly sat back down and took a big sip of my martini. Why did everything Mr. Darcy did make me want to drink inordinate amounts of alcohol?

"So, William tells me that you're are a nurse," Fritz said. He smiled kindly. He was a handsome man with graying hair and an easy smile. He had kind brown eyes that crinkled as he spoke, indicating that he was always smiling.

"I am," I said, doing my best to stay calm. It was easier if I focused on Fritz and not on Mr. Darcy. "I work in the Cardiac ICU."

"That must be very difficult work," Fritz replied. "My father had a heart attack a few years ago, and it was the ICU nurses that kept him alive. They became family to us as he recovered. It's an amazing profession."

A genuine smile slowly replaced my forced one. "Thank you. I love my work, so it's always nice to hear others appreciate it too."

I decided I liked Fritz a lot more than I liked Mr. Darcy right now.

"And Jane, what do you do?" Fritz asked, smiling at Jane.

"I work in art conservation at the art museum," Jane replied. "I specialize in postmodern paintings."

"You work in art?" Fritz's smile grew wider. "William and I have a friend that would love you. He loves art. I should really have you meet him."

I looked over to see Mr. Darcy giving Fritz a death stare. Mr. Darcy had daggers shooting out of his blue eyes. Fritz managed to read Mr. Darcy better than Jane read me, and at least gave him a confused look.

"Would either of you like another drink?" Mr. Darcy asked, standing up quickly.

"I would love one," I replied. My martini was gone and given that I was sitting next to a man I loathed, I needed another.

"I never did get my first one," Fritz announced with a laugh. "I was distracted by beautiful ladies."

Jane smiled at him. "I'll take another as well, please."

"I'm going to go to the bar," Mr. Darcy told the table. "Fritz, would you mind helping me carry them back?"

"I'd like to help," Jane said with a helpful smile.

"She's steadier than I'll be," Fritz replied with a chuckle. "This bum knee of mine always seems to cause me to spill my drinks."

"As you wish," Mr. Darcy replied. He sent a stern look to Fritz as Jane carefully folded her napkin and left it on her chair. Together, she and Mr. Darcy went to pick up drinks.

"I must say, it's wonderful to finally meet you," Fritz told me once Mr. Darcy and Jane were at the bar. "William has spoken very highly of you."

"He has?" I couldn't hide my surprise. That was rather shocking to me, considering that Mr. Darcy never gave me that feeling.

"You must have really made an impression on him," Fritz continued with a nod. "He's usually rather quiet unless it's about business."

"I have noticed that," I replied. "He doesn't seem to care about much else."

"He can definitely appear that way on the outside," Fritz agreed. "But, he's the most loyal friend I've ever had. There isn't anything he wouldn't do for someone he cares about."

Except apparently pick up a telephone and call a girl, I thought to myself. "Is that so?"

"I don't want to betray his confidence, but I think he rather admires you," Fritz confessed.

"What?" I laughed. "I think you must be confusing me with someone else."

"No, I'm quite sure it's you," he replied. "It's just something in the way he speaks about you. He smiles more."

I shook my head. Fritz had to be older than I thought and suffering from dementia. There was no way that Mr. Darcy spoke of me and smiled.

"I find that very interesting," I said diplomatically. I took a sip of water. "He didn't happen to tell you what happened a couple of nights ago?"

Like perhaps why he felt it was acceptable not to call, text, send a carrier pigeon? Why was it okay in his mind to sleep with me and then never contact me? Especially when he acts all happy to see me two days later?

Fritz thought for a moment. "He said he had to do a difficult thing," he said slowly. "Something that was the right thing to do, even if he didn't want to."

I did my best to keep my face straight and not give away anything. Was I the hard but difficult thing? I seemed to remember him pulling off my clothes without too much moral struggle.

"What was it?" I asked. My hands twisted at the napkin in my lap. I had to know now.

Fritz glanced over at the bar. Mr. Darcy and Jane were waiting for their drinks and having what appeared to be a pleasant enough conversation.

"A friend of his was in a bad relationship," Fritz said quietly. "It was rather one-sided and William had to help his friend see it. The girl was a gold digger, and completely uninterested in anything but his money."

My stomach started to twist as I put together the pieces.

"Did you get a name?" I asked.

"Not the girl's," Fritz replied. He glanced back over at Mr. Darcy.

"The friend, was it Charles Bingley?" I asked. The words tasted sour and slimy in my mouth.

"I shouldn't say," Fritz replied, but the look on his face was plain as day. It was Charles, and the only person that could be considered a "gold-digger" was Jane.

"It *was* him. It was Charles Bingley," I confirmed. Fritz didn't deny it.

I looked over at the bar where Jane was smiling and helping Mr. Darcy pick up the drinks. She was smiling at the man who had decided she wasn't worthy of the love of her life.

Red hot fury filled me. I could barely see straight I was so angry. Wrath seethed and boiled in my stomach and I felt like I might hurl it all up if I even opened my mouth.

Mr. Darcy was a monster. Not only did he screw me and not care, but he also cheated Wickham out of his inheritance, and now he'd destroyed my best friend's love and happiness. Any good points he might have once had with me were completely and utterly demolished.

I couldn't stay in the restaurant with him. I didn't want to be on the same planet, let alone the same continent with him after what he'd done. If he came back to the table, I was likely to stab him with my fork. I knew I was out of control and I needed to get myself away from him.

I grabbed my phone and pretended to check the screen.

"I'm so sorry, Fritz," I said, managing to keep my voice light and even, despite the fact that I wanted to scream like a demon. "There's an emergency and Jane and I need to get home right away."

"Oh dear, I hope everything is okay." Fritz's kind face filled with worry. I felt sorry for him. He didn't know that his boss was a monster.

"I'm sure it will be," I told him, standing up and gathering my things. I grabbed Jane's things too. "Please excuse us."

I walked away from the table, not caring if I was being rude or not. All I could see was red.

I grabbed the drinks from Jane and set them down on the bar, spilling most of them. Mr. Darcy could afford it. "We're leaving."

Jane looked at me completely confused as she looked back and forth between me and the drinks. "What? Why?"

"We aren't staying," I growled, grabbing her arm and manhandling her toward the exit.

"Elizabeth? What's going on?" Mr. Darcy asked, confusion twisting his handsome features. He held a martini in each hand.

"Screw you," I hissed at him. I hated that white-hot tears stung at my eyes. I was so angry I could barely see. I ran into a bar stool and just kicked it away, not caring about the fact that it was going to leave a bruise or that we were in a fancy restaurant.

I just wanted out.

I ran for the door, pulling Jane behind me as she shouted an apology to a man who didn't deserve one.

Chapter 13

"Okay, seriously Lizzie?" Jane followed me into our apartment, finally getting frustrated with my lack of words on the subway. "If you aren't going to tell me what's going on, then I have no idea what to do to help."

I slammed the front door hard enough to make the walls shake. "I don't want to talk about it right now," I told her. I vibrated with an uncontrolled fury that I was afraid I was going to unleash on her. "Go to your yoga class."

Frustration filled Jane's face at not being able to help me. "You pull us out of a fancy restaurant and fume the whole way home," she said, putting her hands on my shoulders. "Come on, talk to me. Maybe I can help."

I shrugged her hands away. "You can't help," I told her, doing my best not to sound cruel. "And I don't want to tell you because it will just make things worse."

"That's exactly why you should tell me," Jane reasoned.

"Go to the gym. You have your yoga class that you love," I replied. She didn't move, so I sighed. "I'll tell you when you get home, okay? I just need to cool down a little bit first."

"Are you mad at me?" Jane asked, her big eyes concerned.

"Oh, no, Jane!" I shook my head hard. "Just the opposite."

Jane chewed on her cheek for a moment before going to her room and grabbing her gym bag with her yoga gear.

"I want you to promise you'll tell me when I get back," Jane said.

"I will," I replied, making an X across my chest as promise. Jane still looked torn about leaving me alone.

"Oh, good. You guys are home," Lydia announced, coming into the living room. "Hey, Lizzie, can I borrow a couple of hundred dollars?"

"What?" I felt like I was living in crazy town today.

"It's not a good time to ask, Lydia," Jane cautioned.

"Why in the world do you need money?" I asked Lydia.

"Wickham found out about this party where a bunch of famous photographers will be at," she explained. "I said I could cover the cost of admission."

"Lydia!" I rubbed my temples. This was the last thing I wanted to deal with right now. "What did you tell him? You don't have any money!"

"I told him I had some inheritance money," Lydia replied with a shrug. "Listen, it's not a big deal. This was just an opportunity I thought I should take."

"I don't care about the photo thing." I took a deep breath. "I care about you lying to Wickham that you have money!"

Lydia rolled her eyes. "It doesn't matter. Just go with it. I'll get more parts if I say I can afford *not* to get them. Understand?"

"No, no I don't understand." My head was ready to explode.

"You know what, I'll lend you the money." Jane went and put her arm around Lydia, saving her from me. "Lizzie's having a rough day, so just tell me about this amazing opportunity you found on the way to the gym."

"Okay, Jane." Lydia grinned at her.

"Grab your stuff, and we'll head out," Jane told her. "And remember an umbrella. It's starting to rain."

I watched as Lydia grabbed her gym bag by the front door and the proceeded to take my umbrella. I didn't have the energy to yell at her. I knew if I did, I would just end up exploding at my sister. I didn't want to take my frustration out on her. She didn't deserve the level of rage I was currently holding back.

"So, this is the real deal," Lydia told Jane as they went out into the hallway. "I'm so excited."

Their voices disappeared as I shut the door behind them. I pressed my forehead against the wood of the door, feeling the cool grain against my skin. Everything felt hot.

The world was spinning too fast for me to hold onto. I prided myself on being able to think on my feet. It was a critical skill for me to have as a nurse, but right now I couldn't do it. Mr. Darcy had me dizzy and off balance.

I knew that if he walked in right now and kissed me, I'd melt. I'd fall into that kiss all over again. My sanity and all decision making abilities were gone when it came to him. I didn't know why, but he had this effect on me that I couldn't deny.

I hated him for it. I hated that I wasn't in control of my emotions or libido when he was around. I hated that even after learning all the awful things he'd done, I still wanted to crawl into his bed and have his hands touch me again.

I stood in the middle of my living room, hating Mr.

Darcy and hating myself. I wasn't quite sure who I hated more at that particular moment.

I couldn't stay here. All I wanted to do was hit things, and I knew that neither Jane nor Lydia would appreciate me breaking up the house. So, I grabbed my raincoat since Lydia had my umbrella, and headed out to walk. I would walk to the park and burn off the angry energy so I could think. It sounded like a good plan in my head.

Outside the rain came down in sheets. Cold, wet, and gray were the only adjectives to describe the world, and I was okay with that. It matched my mood: miserable. I knew the rain would probably turn to snow sometime tonight. Maybe a fresh coat of white would make the world look bright again.

I let myself wander the city instead of going to the park. The park had too much beauty, and I wanted the raw gray buildings. I looked inside the various glass windows to see happy people drinking and eating. I watched as they smiled as they made their purchases and I let myself envy them.

They didn't have to deal with Mr. Darcy.

I walked along the barren sidewalks, enjoying the emptiness of the city. The usual crowds were tucked safely inside as I stomped my way through the rain. No one bothered me because there was no one outside to bother.

Until I heard my name.

"Elizabeth."

I froze at his voice, my traitorous body already warming at his call.

He ran across the street to get to me, rain dripping out of his dark hair. He didn't have an umbrella or even a coat. All he wore was his expensive suit jacket, which I was sure was now ruined.

"Elizabeth," he repeated as he closed the distance between us. "I've been looking everywhere for you."

He kissed me, sending glorious heat radiating through every nerve and making my knees go weak. It was everything I remembered in his touch and more. Anger managed to burn through the heat of his touch, igniting me in a different way. I pushed him away, suddenly hot with wrath.

"You didn't call," I spat out, wiping my hand across my mouth. My hood had fallen off during the kiss, and now my hair dripped with the cold rain.

"I needed to see you," he replied. "I wanted to tell you in person."

I crossed my arms, now angry, cold, and wet. My hands were damp now from pushing him, and the cold was biting. I had no idea how he was standing in the pouring rain and not shivering.

"Come here," he said, stepping under the awning of the closest shop. It was the coffee place we'd met at accidentally the other day. Inside people waited in line for hot coffee. It was busy on this cold, wet night.

"What do you want?" I asked, joining him, but keeping my distance. It was nice not to be directly in the rain.

"This isn't how I planned it." He ran a hand through his dark hair, sending droplets of water flying.

I sighed with annoyance and stepped away to go back to the rain, but he caught my elbow and pulled me back under the awning.

"I know you aren't wealthy, that you have no idea what it takes to be a part of my world," he told me. "I know I could have anyone. Any supermodel, heiress, or actress. I could have women more beautiful and accomplished than you in a heartbeat."

I just stared at him, unsure of why I was being insulted. Apparently, I wasn't beautiful or accomplished.

He swallowed hard and set his shoulders. "But I don't want them. I want you," he said. It wasn't soft or kind. It sounded more like he was giving me a job I didn't really deserve. "I don't know why, but I want you."

"What?" I asked, pushing some wet hair out of my face. Inside the coffee shop, I could see a couple of patrons looking at the two crazy people talking outside in the rain. "What do you want me for?"

"I'm willing to take the risk that you may just be after my money," he continued. "My family will disapprove, but for the first time in my life, I don't care."

"I don't understand," I told him, completely lost.

He fixed his serious blue eyes on me. "I love you."

If someone had told me the sky was made of lemon meringue pie, I would have believed them over what I just heard Mr. Darcy said.

"Is this a joke?" I asked him. "Are you serious?"

"Very serious," he said softly. He took a step forward and put his hands on my shoulders, peering into my face with unjustified hope. "Please, say that you feel something for me, too."

I pulled back from his touch. "Oh, I feel something, but it is very far from love."

Confusion and something that might even be mistaken for hurt crossed his face, but I knew better than that. He had to be playing some sort of game with me.

"You honestly think that this was the way to tell me you love me?" I asked. I wasn't cold anymore. I was livid.

"This wasn't what I planned," he said looking around at the rain. "This isn't how I planned to tell you."

"No, not the rain," I corrected. "*I can have anyone. Any*

supermodel, heiress, or actress. I could have women more beau-
tiful and accomplished than you in a heartbeat,' I repeated,
mocking his accent. I felt like I was getting pretty good at it
by now.

He opened his mouth but didn't say anything.

"That's not how you tell someone that you care about
them," I told him. My voice was raising without me meaning
to, and people inside the coffee shop were now looking out
at the two of us. I consciously took a breath to try and keep
my cool. It wasn't working very well. "That's how you tell
people that you *don't* want them."

"Elizabeth..."

"No, that's not even the half of it." I was mad now. Steam
should have been coming off my wet hair I was so hot. "You
didn't call. You didn't even bother saying goodbye the other
night. Who does that?"

He managed to look slightly chagrined. "It was important business," he replied. "It couldn't wait."

"Right. And it's been so pressing that you couldn't pick
up the phone for two days?" I asked. "Your phone doesn't
have texting ability? You somehow lost the knowledge of
how to use a piece of paper and write a note?"

He took a step back.

"You're right," he admitted. "That was impolite of me."

"Impolite?" I barked an incredulous laugh. "Impolite is
using the wrong fork at dinner. You slept with me and didn't
have the decency to say a word after. You just left."

"I had business." He crossed his arms. "Anything else?"

His haughty arrogance at being called out pissed me off.
This was the time to apologize. To tell me that he was
incredibly sorry and that it would never happen again. But
he wouldn't do that. He couldn't do that. He was a smug,

rich, asshole who somehow thought this was what love looked like.

"Yes, yes I actually do," I told him. "You destroyed my sister."

"What?" He managed to sound surprised.

"You told Charles that Jane wasn't interested in him," I said, keeping my voice low for Jane's sake. "She's heartbroken. I know that you said something to him. You want to deny it?"

"No," he replied. "I don't. She didn't want him. It was obvious."

"Oh my god." I nearly turned and walked right then, but I had to understand how he could do such a terrible thing. "Why in the world would you think that?"

"The pictures from the club," he replied. "She's leaning away from him in every one. She looks like she's about to be sick just being there with him. Her body language was unmistakable."

"No, her body language was that she hates crowds," I corrected. "She hates going out to public places, but she was there at that club because he *asked* her. She did it to make him happy."

"She certainly could have fooled me," he snapped back.

"Obviously she did." I was out of control with anger. "And the fact that you called her a gold-digger?"

"I wasn't wrong," he replied. "He has money, and she wants it."

"You are incredibly wrong," I informed him. "Just because he has more money than she does, does not mean she wanted his."

Anger flickered in his blue eyes. "I saw how she looked at those art pieces at the auction," he growled. "She wanted them, and using him was the easiest way to get them. She wanted his money."

"She wanted them because she loves art," I yelled at him. "It's her entire world. If you had actually watched the two of them for three seconds, you'd see that they both wanted those paintings!"

I was breathing hard now, but I wasn't done.

"And what about Wickham?" I asked.

The flicker of anger turned to a full flame in his eyes. "What about him?"

"You ruined him," I snarled. "You stole his inheritance. You wanted to keep your precious business all to yourself, and you stole his rightful share from him. Just like you stole Charles from Jane. You don't care about anyone but yourself! You're nothing but a selfish pig!"

Mr. Darcy took a step back, staggering as if I'd struck him. He stared at me for a moment. "So that's what you think?"

"Yes." I raised my chin defiantly. I knew I could make this less painful. I knew that I could be kind and docile, but I didn't want to be. I felt spiteful and full of vengeance. "From the moment I met you, you've been arrogant, elitist, and uncaring of anyone. I couldn't love you, even if I tried. You're money's not even worth that."

He blinked twice as rainwater ran down his hair and into his face. He looked away and back to me. I made sure to stand strong. I wasn't backing down. He deserved this and so much worse.

I met his gaze, but his eyes were guarded now. The loss of their openness hurt more than I expected, especially when paired with a twinge of guilt for being so cruel in my delivery. I wasn't about to back down, though.

"I apologize," he said softly. "Excuse me for interrupting your evening. I won't bother you again."

He looked me over as if memorizing my face for one last time before disappearing into the dark of the rainy street.

My shoulders heaved as if I had just run a mile rather than just standing there. I looked over to see faces in the window watching us. The entire coffee shop was staring at us. One industrious man was even recording our argument. I wondered how many hits on YouTube I would get for this.

I considered storming in there and slamming his phone into the ground, and while satisfying, it would be a waste of time. It was probably already uploaded.

Besides, it wouldn't matter anyway. Mr. Darcy and I were through, even though we'd never even really began. If we had been in some sort of relationship, it was over now.

Something inside me ached. The adrenaline was wearing off, and my anger was cooling. I shivered and pulled up my hood. I didn't have that white-hot rage powering me anymore, and I was cold inside and out.

I walked out into the rain, more confused than when I'd started walking. Only now, I also wasn't sure if my face was wet with tears or rain.

Chapter 14

"*A*re you okay, Liz?"

I startled and looked up to see one of the CICU night nurses standing in front of me. Her hand rested on my shoulder, and she looked concerned.

"What?" I shook myself, still lost in thought.

"You're only half dressed, and your shift ended twenty minutes ago," she said gently. "Are you okay?"

I looked around the changing area. I was still in the CICU locker room after my shift. I'd managed to put on jeans, but I still wore my scrub top. I'd been sitting on a changing bench with my blue scrub pants in my hands staring into nothingness.

"Oh." I did my best to smile and shake my head like it was nothing. "Just a lot on my mind."

"Okay." My co-worker paused and took a careful breath. "I saw the video. If you need someone to talk to, just let me know. Men suck."

I nodded. "Thanks."

"Okay. Have a good night," she said, heading back out of the locker room. I stared at the closed door behind her, hating and loving the silence of the changing area. The video of Mr. Darcy and I arguing had gone viral, as a woman screaming at a billionaire was likely to do. Luckily, it was hard to make out what we were saying, so most people just thought I was nuts. I just hoped that some new cute cat video would come along and save me from my misery.

I finished getting dressed and headed out of the hospital and to the subway. The train ride home was uneventful, which was good since I was on autopilot anyway. Today, I was just the sad, lonely woman on the train. Nothing strange about that in New York City.

I headed out of the subway to find the night sky dark. Or as dark as it could be this far in the city. I found myself wishing for stars if only to make a wish, but they were all drowned out by the bright city lights.

"Ms. Elizabeth Bennet?" A voice called out from my building as I approached. I paused, reaching for my pepper spray.

"Yes?"

"I have a letter for you." A man with a bike helmet reached into his satchel and pulled out an envelope. I could clearly read the lettering on his bike messenger uniform as he handed me the letter and then rode off to deliver his next package.

I watched him for a moment before looking down at the letter. I'd never had anything delivered by bike messenger before and didn't know who would send me something like this. All that was on the envelope was my name in a tight, neat script.

I headed inside and tapped the button for the elevator. Luckily, I was the only person riding up tonight, so I was able to open the envelope by myself. I wasn't sure what I was expecting, but given the way my week had gone, I didn't want an audience for anything right now.

I pulled out a neatly typed letter with an Oceania Airlines symbol emblazoned on the top. I nearly dropped it.

DEAR ELIZABETH,

I wanted to apologize and explain myself. I knew that I would only hurt you by coming to your home, so I am sending you this letter. It's what I should have done in the first place.

MY BREATH CAUGHT. I thought about throwing it directly in the trash. I didn't want to hear from him. Yet, I couldn't let go of the paper. I had to read it.

I WANTED to address the issues that we spoke of. I do not wish you to think ill of me and would very much like to explain myself.

The first matter I'd like to clarify is George Wickham.

My father loved George as a son. George even took my father's last name. When my father died, he left George a generous inheritance that I never disputed. I often thought that he deserved more. My father left George a trust fund to be paid out over the course of the next fifty years. He would never have to work. My father did this because George had stated on numerous occasions that he did not wish to work in the airline business.

About a year after my father's death, George had the payment changed to a lump sum. I did not fight this, despite it being against my father's wishes. George proceeded to lose the entirety of his money in two years. He then asked me for more, which I refused.

Upon my refusal, he attempted to steal my sister's trust fund using a loophole in the language for its disbursement. Luckily, my lawyers were able to prevent this and my sister retained full rights to her inheritance. In doing this though, he betrayed my entire family.

He has since changed his name back to his mother's maiden name to distance himself from me.

As for your sister, I believed I was doing the right thing. Charles had a previous relationship that nearly destroyed his company when his wife attempted to take over half. Luckily, an infidelity clause spared Charles from losing everything he has worked so hard to build.

I am now very protective of him.

For misjudging your sister, I am most sorry. Your sister did not deserve to be judged based on another's mistakes.

I hope that this clarifies our conversation from the other day. As I said before, I never meant to hurt you, and for that, I apologize.

YOURS,

William Darcy

MY HANDS SHOOK SO HARD I could barely read the last few sentences of his letter. I looked inside the envelope to see he had included several newspaper articles. One was a picture of Jane at Lux. Everyone else was leaning in, and given the angle of the picture, it looked like she was trying to lean away from Charles.

Without knowing Jane and her dislike of photographs, I could understand how someone might think she didn't like him. The picture certainly gave that impression.

The next newspaper article was from a few years ago. A

picture of Wickham pushing away the camera dominated the page with the headline, "George Darcy Filing For Bankruptcy." His hair was longer, but it was definitely the man we knew as Wickham.

Everything Mr. Darcy had said was true.

I walked like a zombie out of the elevator and to the door of our apartment. My hands moved the keys, but my mind was on the letter.

What was I going to do?

I couldn't call and apologize. I'd made too much of a show of telling him how terrible he was. I was so self-righteous in the video. Now I looked like a fool. I couldn't bring myself to admit publicly just how wrong I had been.

I'd burned the bridge between the two of us and then set off some explosives just to make sure it was impassible. If I were Mr. Darcy, I certainly wouldn't forgive me.

"Lizzie!" Lydia shouted as I walked in the door. "I got a gig!"

She jumped up and ran over to me, excitement sparkling in her brown eyes. I set my purse down near the door and simply nodded. I wanted to be happy for her, but I just couldn't seem to make my face show it.

Luckily, Lydia didn't seem to notice. "It's just standing in front of another car dealership and looking pretty."

"That's great," I mumbled.

"The only bad part is that I'm not getting paid," she told me with a shrug. "Well, I mean, I am. It's just that Wickham is using the money to get me more jobs. I told him that was fine since I'm loaded."

"That's nice," I replied, shuffling toward my room. I just wanted to lay down. I didn't want to deal with Lydia's issues today. I just couldn't. Not after the letter.

"See, Jane?" Lydia stuck her tongue out at Jane in the kitchen. "She doesn't care. It's *fine*."

"I still say it isn't, Lydia," Jane replied. She frowned at me, waiting for me to jump in and agree with her. I was just two steps from my bedroom door, so I didn't say a word. I just opened it and went inside.

I could hear the two of them yelling at one another as I shut myself in my room. Their words just jumbled and were noise in my head as I sagged against my door and slowly fell to the floor. My hands still gripped the letter and newspaper clippings like they were the only real thing left in the world.

I didn't know what to do.

A sob escaped me followed by hot tears that I couldn't explain.

Chapter 15

"*Holy* crap." Jane stared at me with big eyes and an open mouth. "Wickham seemed so nice."

"I know," I replied, setting down my breakfast bowl of ice cream on the counter to add a little more chocolate sauce. I needed chocolate after last night.

Lydia was off at her photo-shoot this morning, so I'd told Jane about the letter. I only told her the part about Wickham, though. Telling her that she'd lost the love of her life because Mr. Darcy thought she was a gold-digger wasn't going to do her any good.

Jane shook her head before going back to scrubbing the oven. Jane claimed she was over Charles, but the fact that our kitchen was the cleanest it had ever been since the 1970's said otherwise. He wasn't answering her calls or messages. She said it wasn't a big deal, but I didn't believe her. She'd even gotten a toothbrush out to clean the grout between the kitchen tiles. She'd already done it to the bathroom. Twice.

If I told her that this was all because of Mr. Darcy's misunderstanding, she'd have to go on another cleaning bender. And, in this little apartment, we were running out of things to clean.

"I checked out Mr. Darcy's story about him," I said. I pulled out my phone and handed the search results I'd found to Jane.

"Holy crap," she repeated, looking through the images.

Everything about Wickham that Mr. Darcy said was true. Searching for George Darcy brought up hundreds of images of him partying and living it up. He'd apparently even capsized a million dollar yacht in Belize.

Then came the pictures and articles of him declaring bankruptcy. The pictures went from fun and expensive to sad and poor quicker than I had expected. He had inherited *a lot* of money.

"It's actually kind of sad," Jane remarked, handing me back my phone. She pushed some hair out of her face before returning to the oven with her scrub brush.

"Yeah," I agreed. "But what do I tell Lydia?"

"What can you tell her?" Jane asked, leaning thoughtfully against the oven door. "Even if you give her the letter and all the evidence, she won't let him go. He's her agent. She's signed contracts, and honestly, he's the only thing she talks about."

"I know," I replied, taking a big spoonful of chocolate sauce. "It'll destroy her."

Jane nodded, and I sighed.

"At least she doesn't have much money," I said after a moment. "She keeps telling him she does, but he'll figure out the truth sooner or later. She can't be of much use to him."

"Yeah," Jane agreed. "And don't worry, I'm not lending her any more money. Not if it's just going to go to that scumbag."

"Wow, Jane," I said impressed. "I rarely hear you say anything negative about anyone."

She shrugged. "You just haven't heard what I say about you when you aren't around." She looked up and winked at me with a laugh.

I rolled my eyes at her and chuckled. I took another bite of ice cream and a bigger bite of chocolate.

"We'll tell her after New Years," I said, thinking out loud. "He won't hurt her, and there's not much he can do to her. I mean, what's the worst that can happen? If he thinks she has money, he'll be good to her."

"New Years is good," Jane agreed, nodding. Her blonde ponytail bounced up and down with the motion. "New Years will be a fresh start for all of us."

My heart ached a little at the way she said it. Charles had hurt her, and it was Mr. Darcy's fault, though done with the best intentions. The whole situation made me sad, so I ate some more ice cream and chocolate.

Jane went back to cleaning the oven, and I looked over the images and articles I'd found on Wickham. I was scrolling down when an article caught my eye. It had caught the name Georgiana Darcy up in my search for George Darcy. I only hesitated a second before clicking on her name.

Georgiana was Mr. Darcy's younger sister. I remembered him saying something about her, but now I knew her name. She was much younger than I expected, nearly half the age of her older brother. I could see why he would be protective of his teenage sister.

I clicked further down to find a picture of Mr. Darcy and Georgiana standing in front of a St. George's Hospital when they opened up a new wing last year. She was so thin and frail next to him, yet so many of their facial features were shared.

I read further. Mr. Darcy had donated the entire wing. It was to be a cancer center with a specialty in leukemia. I looked back at the picture of the thin, frail girl that smiled like Mr. Darcy and felt my stomach twist.

"What's wrong?" Jane asked, looking up at me. "You gasped."

"Mr. Darcy's little sister had leukemia," I replied, reading the article as quickly as possible. The more I read, the more I knew I had pegged him wrong. "He not only donated a whole hospital wing to St. George's, but he also added a new surgery center, and he runs a charity for kids who can't afford their cancer treatments."

"That sounds like a lot of money," Jane replied.

"Yeah," I agreed. I closed my eyes and banged my head on the counter twice before looking over at her. "I called him a selfish pig."

"Ouch," Jane winced. "You okay?"

"Am I okay that I called one of the leading cancer philanthropists a selfish pig?" I shrugged and then banged my head again. "I'm an idiot."

"We're all idiots in love," Jane replied softly. My head went straight up, and I looked straight at her.

"What?"

"Oh, not you," Jane clarified shaking her head. "The expression just popped into my head. I was thinking about selfish pigs. I know you slept with him, but that doesn't mean love. That's lust. Apparently, lots of men confuse the two."

I raised my eyebrows, waiting for her to admit that she was thinking about Charles and how he was a selfish pig for letting her go. She just looked at me and shrugged.

"So what do I do?" I asked her. "I'm in the wrong here."

Jane thought for a moment. "Do you plan on spending time with him?" she asked. "Do you want to sleep with him again?"

"God, no," I answered a little too quickly. My body did, but I knew it wasn't going to happen. This time, Jane raised her eyebrows at me. "I mean, it was good, but, I don't like him or anything. Lust, remember?"

"Then just stay out of his way," Jane advised. "If you do see him, apologize then. But, you two don't exactly run in the same social circles, so I don't see that happening."

"Yeah," I agreed, staring into my ice cream. "I'm beneath him."

"Hey, I didn't say that," Jane replied firmly. "Money isn't everything."

"You should tell him that," I told her. I took a bite of ice cream.

"Are you sure you're okay?" Jane asked. "You seem really upset over this, especially if he doesn't mean anything to you."

"He doesn't," I assured her. I hated that my stomach twisted as I said it. "Why would I? He's a spoiled, arrogant little rich boy."

"You forgot hoity-toity and Richy McRich pants," Jane replied dryly. "I think those are the words you used last time."

"And British," I added. "He's *so* British."

Jane chuckled and stood up to hug me. She smelled like oven cleaner. "You'll be fine."

"You're right," I told her after she squeezed me. "I'm not likely to run into him again, so it's not something I need to worry about."

Jane nodded, then paused. "What about the Christmas party?"

"The hospital one?" I asked. I shrugged. "He won't be there. It's the wrong hospital."

"You're right," Jane agreed. "He wouldn't go unless he likes to torture himself." She thought about it for a moment. "He's not that kind of billionaire, is he?"

We both dissolved into a fit of giggles.

Chapter 16

"*H*e won't be here, he won't be here, he won't be here," I chanted softly as the taxi drove me to the hotel. If I said it enough times, then I knew it would have to come true.

I knew I was right. He was part of a different hospital. There was no reason for him to be here. Still, there was a worry in the pit of my stomach.

I looked out the window to see a beautiful old brick building come into sight. I could see why he'd picked this hotel.

The annual holiday hospital party was being held at one of the fancy hotels on the other side of the park from me. It was close, but I would have to take a cab or walk across the park at night. That wasn't really a problem until I found out that Mr. Darcy was known for staying in the penthouse suite of this particular hotel. It was his preferred location when in New York. Because that was how my life worked.

I considered not going to the party. I considered simply returning the gorgeous dress I'd rented and staying in my apartment eating chocolate ice cream and watching lame

Christmas movie specials where everyone ended up happy and celebrating the magic of Christmas.

But Jane told me no. And Lydia told me no. They both told me that I had to get over myself and go to the party. Lydia even made sure I had the right shoes laid out this morning. She had left the house early, so I didn't have time to thank her.

I asked Jane to come with me, but she said she was partied out. She was going to a drawing class. I was on my own, but I was going to the party whether I liked it or not.

So, now I was just hoping that either Mr. Darcy wasn't here this week, or if he was, he would decide to just stay up in his room.

As long as he did that, I could enjoy this night out with my co-workers. Tonight was for anyone and everyone who worked at the hospital to get dressed up and enjoy a party. There was supposed to be live music, free food, and a cash bar. If it was terrible, I could easily leave early.

The taxi pulled up to the building, and I took a deep breath.

"He won't be here, he won't be here," I told myself, putting on a confident face. With more courage showing than I felt, I walked inside.

I found the ballroom hosting our party easily enough. The hospital decorated everything with silver tinsel, and I felt like I'd stepped into a giant, shiny snow-globe. The band on stage was playing classic rock songs that felt odd at a holiday party until I noticed that the lead drummer was the head of cardiac surgery. The front singer was my favorite anesthesiologist. It was the perfect band for the party, even if they weren't the traditional holiday songs.

I grinned and walked around. Coworkers waved, and I caught up with nurses from other floors. Even if Mr. Darcy did come down from his penthouse, he wouldn't come to this party. I was safe here. I began to relax and enjoy myself.

I let myself wander and enjoy the decorations. One of the walls was covered in news articles from the year that had something to do with the hospital or medicine. Many of the stories were about families and finding diagnoses or cures, but one caught my eye.

It was a picture of children meeting Santa. It would have been a normal Santa picture, except every child had an IV pole or wore a PICC line. Medical equipment dominated the background. These were not healthy children, but their smiles were so big and bright at meeting Santa that I couldn't help but look.

That's when I saw him. It was just a small picture, but Mr. Darcy was there, sitting on the floor playing a game with a child in a hospital gown. I nearly didn't recognize him with the smile on his face. It was strange to see the man who never smiled look so happy.

The caption underneath the picture read: All Toys Donated by Oceanic Airlines to the Georgiana Cancer Wing.

I stared at the smiling man in the background of the picture. Could I go anywhere without being reminded of him? Was it possible for me to go two days without seeing the good in him that I had so obviously missed?

It was as if Fate were taunting me. He was a good man if I had just opened my eyes and given him a real chance.

I sighed and walked away. I didn't need to be reminded that I'd been wrong. I didn't need yet another reminder that I had misjudged him so badly. He was still a pompous jerk. He was just a kind and charitable pompous jerk.

The sound of piano music in another room caught my attention. The classic rock doctor band was taking a break, so the soft clarity of the piano tugged at me. It was definitely a live performance rather than the canned music playing over the speakers.

I followed the sound to the next ballroom to find a young woman sitting at a giant piano. She had the most radiant smile on her face as her fingers made music, and I couldn't help but stand at the edge of the room and listen.

The young woman suddenly stopped and looked up, noticing she had an audience.

"Please, don't stop," I begged, stepping into the empty room. "You play wonderfully."

The young woman smiled and blushed. "Thank you."

"You should be playing in there," I said, motioning to the party room. "I think they'd all appreciate your playing."

The woman smiled again. She was thin and delicate with big green eyes that looked tired. Her dark hair was trimmed to a short pixie cut that accentuated her petite frame and thin features. She couldn't have been more than eighteen or so, but there was something in her eyes that made me think she was older than her years.

"Thanks," the young woman replied. She sat at the piano and gave me a conspiratorial grin. "I'm actually supposed to be at that party, but I don't know anyone there."

"So you're hiding in here?" I asked, taking another step closer. She seemed familiar to me, but I couldn't place from where. She had a soft British accent that fit well with her playing piano. It all seemed very smart.

"Yup. I am totally hiding," she admitted. "Don't tell my brother."

"Not a word," I promised, crossing the small room. "Will you keep playing?"

"Sure," she said with an easy shrug. "Do you play? I know a couple of duets."

She scooted over on the bench to give me room to sit. I paused as she smiled at me.

"I haven't played since I was a kid," I told her. "I'm not very good."

"Come sit with me anyway," she replied. "It makes me feel less lonely."

I couldn't say no to a request like that, so I sat beside her as she began to run her fingers over the keys in a simple, yet beautiful song I didn't recognize. I loved watching her fingers make music right before my eyes. It was like magic.

"Well, at least you know someone at the party now," I told her as she slowed her fingers and ended the song. "You know me."

She grinned, her green eyes sparkling. "You work at St. Austen's?"

"I do," I said with a grin. "I'm a nurse there."

"Do you know anyone in the Cardiac ICU?" the young woman asked, her voice excited.

"That's the floor I work on," I replied with a grin. "There's a lot of good people on my floor."

Her fingers picked a new melody, this one light and bright. It made me happy just listening to it.

"I'm Georgiana, by the way," she told me, adding a small flourish to the end of the musical phrase.

I nearly fell off the bench. I should have known.

"Georgiana Darcy?" I asked.

The universe hated me.

"Yeah, how'd you know?" she asked, giving me a friendly grin. She paused, the music stopping suddenly as her grin somehow grew wider. "You must be Elizabeth!"

She turned on the bench and wrapped her arms around me in a giant hug. She was stronger than she looked. Mr.

Darcy's younger sister was sitting next to me and knew my name. This couldn't end well.

"Oh. You know me," I said lamely, unsure of what to do next.

"Only by what my brother has told me," she confessed. "He doesn't say nice things about a lot of people, but he always speaks very highly of you."

I nearly fell off my chair again. "He does?"

She nodded. "I'm so glad to meet you. It's actually one of the reasons I agreed to come to the party in the first place."

"Really?" I still couldn't get over the fact that her brother said nice things about me, not just to one person, but two. Fritz and Georgiana both had heard nice things from me.

"My brother always has to go to these parties," she explained. "I don't like going to them all, but I wanted to meet you. So, when he offered, I came."

"I'm flattered," I told her. I had no idea what I was supposed to say next. I knew I should get up and run as fast as my heels could take me. If she were waiting for her brother, he would be here any moment. The idea of seeing him made my stomach do strange things.

"Is your brother here?" I asked, glancing around the empty room like he might appear in a puff of smoke and surprise me.

"He will be. They expect it, between the presents he has donated and other money. Did you know that he even bid up all the items that nobody was bidding on at the silent auction a couple weeks ago?"

How could I forget the antique journal that he snatched away from me? "You don't say," I said through gritted teeth. "What a gentleman."

She beamed. "He sure is. Right now, he's upstairs on a phone call," she explained. "Something with the merger going on. Catherine has been on him nonstop to make this thing happen."

I seemed to remember Charles mentioning the name Catherine as well.

"Catherine?" I asked. "Who is she?"

"The COO of the company," Georgiana explained. She made a sour face. "She's a terrible human being, but an excellent businesswoman. She has run the company since before Will inherited it."

"Oh," I replied.

She's just here to meet a rich husband, so she doesn't have to work her meaningless job, I remembered Charles repeating, but in a high-pitched old-lady voice that first night at the gala. I had a pretty good idea I didn't like Catherine.

"Sometimes, I think Will spends too much time with her," Georgiana whispered to me. "All she cares about is growing the business even bigger and making sure that no one takes advantage of her or Will. She doesn't care about anyone but her own ego."

"That certainly explains some of the things he's said," I replied with a dry chuckle.

"Did he parrot her to you?" Georgiana shook her head. "I'm working on making him behave more human. He forgets that business isn't all there is to life. Sometimes life should be about dancing and playing the piano."

"Cheers to that," I told her, even though I didn't have a drink. For being as young as she was, she was full of wisdom.

"Have you eaten yet?" Georgiana asked, changing the subject.

"Not yet," I admitted. "Why? Can you hear my stomach growling?"

Georgiana laughed. "No, but they have the best dinner

rolls here. Come on. I'll show you where they keep the good stuff."

She grinned and grabbed my hand, pulling me away from the piano. I could have said no to a tornado with more ease. I had a feeling that Georgiana had the unique talent of being able to get whatever she wanted while making people feel good at the same time.

We made it halfway across the room when the door opened and in walked a gorgeous man in a suit. My heart suddenly dropped and soared at the same time.

"I know you're in here hiding with the piano, Geo," Mr. Darcy said, stepping into the room. He had that same smile from the picture on his face. It quickly faded as soon as he saw me. His feet even stumbled a little bit.

I know mine did.

"Will! Look who I found," Georgiana announced, presenting me with her hands like I was a long-lost treasure. "She's wonderful. I wish you would have introduced us earlier."

I just stood there, unable to form English words. Nothing seemed adequate. Nothing seemed to sound right in my head, so I just stood there, looking up into those blue eyes that loved to give toys to kids with cancer.

"I, um..." Mr. Darcy cleared his throat, and I felt a little better that he didn't know what to say either.

"We were just about to get some food," Georgiana continued, completely oblivious to the strange tension between her brother and me.

"If you two have other plans, I can go," I said quickly. "I'm fine. I don't want to interrupt."

I couldn't help but meet those blue eyes again. I couldn't read if he was angry or sad. He just stared at me, keeping me in the tractor beam of his gaze. I felt so stupid. I wanted to be mad at him, but I couldn't. Not after the letter. Not after seeing the pictures on the wall.

If anything, I felt like the biggest stupid-head in the state.

"No, no other plans," he stammered. A slight pink came into his cheeks. He couldn't seem to look away from me either.

"Okay then, let's go. I'm hungry," Georgiana took my arm and started walking to the door. "I love the rolls they make here. They're amazing. Even when I have my treatments, Will just has an order of them ready because they're the only thing I can keep down. You have to try them."

"Okay," I agreed, nodding along to her easy conversation.

"Keep up, Will," she called back, flashing him a smile as we left the room. I looked back to see him following us. His eyes were only on me.

Chapter 17

*T*wo drinks, some food, and the most amazing dinner rolls I'd ever eaten, and I was having a wonderful evening. It was the most surprising thing to me.

Georgiana never stopped talking, it seemed. She always had something sweet and funny to say, and I was glad. It filled in the awkward silences whenever Mr. Darcy and I didn't know what to say. She kept the conversation smooth and flowing.

He kept watching me, those blue eyes taking in my every movement. To be fair, I kept watching him from the corner of my eye. He looked so handsome sitting with us. His dark hair was combed back, and his suit displayed the strength of his shoulders and trim of his waist.

It helped that I knew exactly what was under that suit, but I knew I would never have that again. Still, every time he glanced over at me, my heart did flip-flops. I had slept with the man, so there was no reason to be nervous around him, yet there I was. I felt like a schoolgirl next to the captain of the football team.

I laughed too hard at his jokes. I smiled too much when

he looked over at me. I tried to come up with something witty or clever to say at every chance, which meant that I sounded like an idiot most every time I opened my mouth. I was giving serious thought to calling Lydia just to get some flirting tips because I was sucking so badly at it.

"I'm going to go get some more of those chocolate strawberries," Georgiana announced, standing up from her seat. She swayed slightly, her thin body struggling with the sudden movement. She wasn't completely healthy yet, and I suspected that her adorable pixie cut was less choice and more about using what hair she had left.

"I'll come with you," I told her, rising up myself.

She shooed me back down. "No, no," she said, shaking her head. "I'll be right back. You stay here."

She flashed me a grin that told me she knew exactly what she was doing leaving the two of us alone.

Unfortunately, I had no idea what to do. And given the awkward silence, neither did Mr. Darcy.

"She's adorable," I finally blurted out. "Your sister, I mean. I mean..." I took a deep breath. How did he fluster me without even saying a word? I smiled at him and tried again. "I'm having a very nice evening. Thank you for letting me join you and your sister."

He smiled, and my heart went into double time.

"Likewise," he replied.

I needed something smart to say. Something that would make him smile at me like that again.

"So, how's the buyout going?" I asked, trying to sound casual. "I saw something about it proceeding as planned in the news the other day."

I suddenly found myself wishing I'd paid more attention to the news story. A patient had been watching it when I came in to check vitals, so I didn't really have that option, but that didn't change me from wishing I had.

"It's going well," he replied. He sounded so calm and smooth. "I'm very pleased with it. We have a meeting tomorrow to finalize everything. I wish everything in my life would work out as well as this did."

The way he looked at me told me he meant me. I swallowed hard and looked down at my hands. This would be a great time to apologize. I knew that I should, yet somehow I couldn't get the words out. My pride was too big.

"I'm glad it's working out for you," I instead told him. It was lame as hell. "I wish you all the success in the world."

"Thank you." A small ghost of a smile flickered across his face. It made me ache to see him smile again.

"Will you be staying in New York after the deal is complete?" I asked, holding my breath. I hoped he was.

"Just until the end of the year," he replied. "Geo loves New York this time of year. Plus, I think she likes getting away from Catherine."

"Your COO?" I asked, making sure I had the right one.

He nodded. "Yes. Our Aunt Catherine looks after Geo when I'm out on business," Mr. Darcy said. "Catherine prefers to stay in London, so Geo takes any opportunity to come with me to New York she can."

"I'm glad she came." I smiled, meaning it. If she hadn't come to the party, I would never have had this wonderful time with her and Mr. Darcy.

I racked my brain, trying to come up with something that we could have a real discussion on. I wanted to keep talking with him all night. I was about to ask him about his flying when Georgiana reappeared.

It was perfect and yet terrible timing.

"I managed to get the last three strawberries," she

announced. "Everything is shutting down. Apparently, the party is ending."

"What?" I looked down in shock at my watch. "It's supposed to go until eleven."

"And it's eleven fifteen," Georgiana informed me. My watch backed her up. How in the world had so many hours gone by without me noticing?

"Oh dear." I quickly pulled out my phone and saw several missed messages. Three were from my ride home. The first said it was time to leave, the second where she was, and then the third that she was leaving without me. There was even a message from Jane asking when I'd be home. I hadn't even noticed them.

"What's wrong?" Mr. Darcy asked, his face concerned.

"My ride home left. She has to work tomorrow, so she left earlier," I explained. I put my phone away and shrugged. "It's not important. I can get a cab really easily."

"I'll take you home." He didn't hesitate. He didn't have to think about it. He just offered.

"You don't have to, Mr. Darcy," I told him, standing up from the table. I doubted he wanted to be stuck with me any longer than he had to be.

"No, I'd like to." His voice was soft. I melted a little bit, even though I wanted to protest a little bit more. The idea of being alone with him was making my heart stutter. As much as I wanted more time with him, what in the world would I say without Georgiana to fill in the big silent parts?

"Good, it's settled then," Georgiana announced before I could tell him no. "My brother will take you home, and I get to see you again. Promise?"

There was no way I could say no to that. "Of course. I'd like that very much."

"Good." She grinned, but the frowned. "Now, why have

you been calling him 'Mr. Darcy' all night? I thought you two knew each other."

"Well, the night I met your brother, I did call him William," I told her. "He corrected me and told me to call him Mr. Darcy."

"William!" Georgiana's accent became much sharper as she smacked her brother on the shoulder. She glared at him before returning to face me. "I apologize for him."

Mr. Darcy's cheeks darkened. "I did do that, didn't I?"

I nodded. "Among other things."

He got up and came to stand before me, his blue eyes focused on me. I was the center of his world, and it was a heady experience. "I am sorry."

My knees went weak, and my heart threatened to go into a-fib. I reached for the table just to keep me upright.

"Me too," I whispered, staring into his eyes. "For everything."

It wasn't as much of an apology as he deserved, but it was at least the start of one. A weight lifted off my shoulders, and I knew I should have apologized a long time ago.

He smiled, lighting up those blue eyes and making my knees tremble a little more.

"You're more than forgiven," he said softly.

"Well that's good," Georgiana said, reminding us that she was still there. She held up a strawberry. "Strawberry for the road?"

I shook my head. "No, thank you."

She shrugged and popped one happily into her mouth. "Good. More for me then."

I gave her a big hug. I couldn't help but like the girl. She was still struggling with her illness, but there was no way she was letting it bring her down. She was a light in this world and reminded me a lot of my grandmother in the best possible way.

The three of us walked into the mostly deserted lobby. I couldn't believe that I'd had such a nice time with the two Darcy siblings that I'd lost all track of time. I would never have thought it possible.

"You go on up to the room," Mr. Darcy told Georgiana as she stifled a yawn. "I'll take Elizabeth home."

"Take your time," she told him as she headed toward the elevator. She waved one last time as I went to retrieve my coat. It was easy to find because it was the last one left.

"You don't really have to take me home," I told Mr. Darcy as he helped me slide on my coat. "It's not far. And a cab is really easy."

"I want to," he replied. "Stop arguing."

I nodded in acquiescence. "As you wish."

He chuckled. The sound was rich and joyful, and it made me look up in surprise. "What's so funny?"

"Submission looks very strange on you," he told me. "You never give in."

"That's a nice way of saying I'm stubborn," I said. He just grinned at me and put his hand on the small of my back to guide me to the valet. His touch, even through my coat, made my stomach flutter and my nerves tingle. I was glad I was wearing a coat, or he would have been able to feel my heat.

The valet jumped to attention as we walked out. "Mr. Darcy, I'll have your car up right away, sir." He took a step and then stopped. "Which one would you like?"

"The red one, please," Mr. Darcy replied.

The valet nodded and took off running. I'd never seen someone move that fast, but then again, I also wasn't worth billions. Or even had a car.

"How many cars do you have here?" I asked, realizing that the valet made it sound like there were multiple.

"Three," he replied with a nonchalant shrug.

"You have three cars in New York City?" I repeated, not quite believing him. "You don't even officially live here."

He shrugged. "I like cars," he told me with a small smile. "Oh, I guess it's four if you count the limo."

"Oh, yes. You can't forget the limo. How silly of you," I said, smiling back at him.

"And a helicopter," he added. "But that's just to beat the traffic."

"And who doesn't need that," I agreed with a giggle. I shook my head in amazement. I didn't have a car. I didn't even technically have a drivers license because I never needed one. The closest I'd ever been to a helicopter was receiving patients on the roof of the hospital, but I'd never actually even been in one.

His world of wealth was very different than mine.

A bright fire-engine red Ferrari pulled up to the valet station, and the valet hopped out. He handed Mr. Darcy the keys, and Mr. Darcy tipped him some money. It looked like a hundred dollar bill.

Mr. Darcy opened the passenger door for me to get in.

"Seriously?" I said, looking at the beautiful sports car. "This is your drive around New York car?"

He just grinned and held out his hand to help me in.

I took his outstretched hand, trying not to flush at the skin to skin connection as I settled into the leather seats. I looked around, trying to take it all in. It was the most beautiful car I'd ever seen. Everything was smooth lines and leather. It even smelled amazing.

I tried not to think about how much a car like this cost. It was probably worth a decade of my salary. I tried to sit with as little of me touching the car as possible so I wouldn't mess anything up.

He closed the door and walked around to the driver's side.

"Yup. Good choice me," I said softly as I watched him pass the front of the car. "Don't date the rich guy. Be awful to him. Call him names. That's a good life choice."

I could have had all of this. If I had said that I loved him back that night in the rain, or even just given him a chance, I could have had a helicopter.

But, I had to be all high and mighty. I had to call him names and act like a child. It was my own fault and I didn't deserve his riches. Besides, I was never after his money. It was just that getting to see it was rather eye-opening.

Mr. Darcy sat down and turned on the car. It hummed quieter than I expected. Then he grinned at me and revved the engine. That was the amazing super fast, powerful engine sound I was expecting.

"Now you're just showing off," I teased him.

"What's the point in having a car like this if you don't show it off a little?" He asked, putting the car into gear and pulling out. The tires squealed as the engine accelerated. I laughed as I was thrown back into the soft leather and my insides were pushed down.

The car was damn fast.

And then, we hit traffic, because we were in New York.

I laughed as he came to a stop at the first traffic light. It didn't matter that we were in the fanciest, fastest car. We still had to follow the flow of traffic.

"Thank you again for taking me home," I said as we waited for the light to change.

He looked over at me and smiled, making my heart flutter. "Of course."

"Do you want to tell me more about your buyout?" I asked. It was going to be an awkward drive home if we didn't have something to fill the silence.

He looked over, evaluating me. "Do you really want to know?"

"I do." I was actually surprised by the fact that I really did.

"My airline is purchasing South Pacific Airway," he began. "They serve primarily the South Pacific in a way we haven't been able to do yet. By combining with them, we'll be able to control twenty percent of all Asian airline traffic."

"Wow, that sounds like a lot," I said. He nodded as he pulled through the light. We were immediately stopped again by traffic.

"It's been a difficult acquisition," he explained. "We are working through the legal issues and making sure that our corporate cultures are compatible. We want to make sure that our companies combine seamlessly on the employee level."

I nodded. "When I was first hired as a new grad, the hospital was merging with another corporation. Everyone was trying to figure out how the new billing systems and pay codes all worked. It was a nightmare. There was a lot of *'but it used to be this way'* being thrown around."

"Exactly." He nodded. "We're trying to minimize that from the top down, which has made the negotiations tedious."

"I would imagine it would make things smoother in the long run, though."

"It should," he agreed. "I intend to learn from my mistakes."

"Mistakes? You made a mistake?" I asked.

"It does happen from time to time," he informed me, smiling as he said it.

I grinned back. "So, what are you changing this time? For your company?"

He hesitated. "Are you sure you want to hear this?"

"Yes," I assured him. "It's actually pretty interesting. I'd love to learn more."

He glanced over at me, his eyes soft like he'd found a treasure. He grinned.

We spent the rest of the ride home discussing various methods of gaining compliance. He listened and nodded when I put forth my experience and he actually liked some of my ideas. For the first time in my life, I actually really enjoyed the traffic and was sad when we arrived at my apartment.

I found myself wanting the night to keep going.

"Thank you again," I told him as he pulled into the parking area for my building. "I had a really nice evening."

"Me too," he replied. He flashed me that soft smile that made my knees buckle.

I hesitated in getting out of the car. I wasn't ready for our conversation to end, especially since I wasn't sure when I'd get to see him again. After this, there was literally no chance of us meeting unless he ended up as a patient, and I didn't want that.

"Would you like to come up for a drink?" I asked. "Jane bought this bottle of wine that she thought I would like, and I can't drink it on my own."

Even in my head, the words sounded lame. It was the best I could do on short notice. I wasn't used to coming up with excuses to bring men home.

He took a small breath and thought for a moment.

He's going to say no, I thought to myself. *He should say no. I've been a total bitch. This was a dumb idea...*

"I'd love to," he replied. I nearly laughed with joy. Excitement and relief filled me, quickly replaced with nerves. I couldn't remember if I'd made my bed this morning and what the state of my bathroom looked like. I hoped Jane was still at her drawing class.

But mostly, I hoped that we actually still had that random bottle of wine.

Chapter 18

*H*e got out and ran around to open my car door. It made me smile and feel important to be treated like a lady. I was a self-sufficient and strong woman, but it was nice to be taken care of too.

I babbled in the elevator about the weather on our way up. It wasn't because I thought the weather would interest him, but more because I was afraid I would want to kiss him if I didn't keep my mouth busy.

Even in the pale neon glow of the elevator, he was the most handsome man I'd ever met in real life. Being in the elevator with him close enough to touch, I could smell his cologne. I remembered the way he made me feel. I could feel myself leaning toward him, wanting to feel that again.

I needed to get a grip on myself and my hormones. I'd hurt him, and I needed to go slow if I wanted to regain any of his trust. I was still surprised that he had agreed to the drink. I didn't want to push my luck too much and kissing him in the elevator would definitely do that.

Relief washed over me as the elevator doors opened and I hadn't done anything I would regret or that would embarrass me. I had kept a respectable distance and had remained appropriate. So far, so good.

I hurried into the hallway, glad to have a little more space to lessen the temptation to touch him.

I knew that I shouldn't feel this attraction. I knew that he had every reason to hate me. Yet, despite it all, he was coming with me, and we were having a lovely evening.

I had no idea how it was going to end. I half wanted it to be in my bed, but the idea terrified me as well. I had no idea what I was doing.

I opened the door to the apartment and held it open.

"Here's my apartment," I announced, feeling dumb. "Please come in."

"Oh, thank god you're home," Jane cried, jumping up from the couch and rushing over. Her face was wet with tears, and her hands shook.

"Jane? What's the matter?" I asked, putting my hands on her shoulders. The poor thing was trembling all over. "What happened?"

Jane's lower lip trembled. "Lydia's run away."

I took a step back in shock and ran directly into Mr. Darcy. He was strong and stable behind me, and it gave me some comfort to know he was there.

"What do you mean, 'run away'?" I asked, my heart already beating hard.

"Lydia ran away with Wickham," Jane explained. "They're in LA. She says he's going to make her famous, and..."

Her voice caught, and she had to take a breath.

"And?" I pressed. I already knew there was nothing good that could come next. Jane didn't fluster easily. Something was very wrong with this trip.

"And I checked with his office," Jane said slowly. "They

fired him two weeks ago. He put a girl in a porno without her consent and took the extra money without telling the company."

"No..." The floor fell out from under me. It was a good thing that Mr. Darcy was behind me or I would have collapsed to the floor. As it was, he had to half carry me over to the couch. My feet didn't seem to know how to work properly. This was the worst possible outcome to this situation.

"I'm so sorry, Lizzie." Jane joined me on the couch and took my hand. "I didn't know what else to do."

"It's not your fault, Jane," I told her. Shock settled on my limbs, heavy and awful. "How did you find out?"

"She left a note," Jane explained. She pulled a small piece of paper out of her pocket. I could see Lydia's handwriting on it. "It only says she's in LA with Wickham for a big role. That's why I called his office."

"She would have left me a note, too," I said, rising to my feet. Mr. Darcy rose with me, making sure I was still steady.

I ran to my room and found a small piece of folded paper on my bed. It struck me as important that I had made my bed this morning, but it didn't matter now.

My hands shook as I picked up the note and read the messy writing.

DEAR LIZZIE,

When you get back, I'll already be in Los Angeles. I don't want you to worry, but this is my big break, and I couldn't have you talk me out of it.

I told Wickham that I wasn't an heiress, just like you asked me to. You were right; I should have told him all along. Now that he knows, he's taking me to Hollywood! He says he has a gig for me there and that it will make me a star.

I had to borrow some of your money to pay for plane tickets, but I promise I'll pay you back once I get the money for this part.

You're going to be so proud of me. I promise.

Love,

Lydia

"STUPID GIRL," I whispered, wiping a tear from my cheek. How could she be so foolish? How could I have not seen this coming?

"Elizabeth?" Mr. Darcy stood in the doorway to my room, waiting for me to tell him to come in. Concern filled his strong features, and those blue eyes wanted to help me.

"What do I do?" I asked him. I felt the tears coming and closed my eyes. "This is bad. This is so bad."

"Let me see," he said gently, taking a step toward me. I handed him the letter and watched his face as he read it. His eyes narrowed, and his brow grew dark. His jaw pulsed with tension as he finished reading it.

"This is my fault," he said softly, his voice low. "If I'd exposed him earlier, she wouldn't be in this situation."

"No," I said, putting my hand on his arm. "This is my fault. You told me what he was. I didn't tell my sister because I didn't want to hurt her. Now, I've hurt her worse. If I had just told her what you told me, this never would have happened."

"Elizabeth, I'd like to help." His voice was soothing as he put a hand on my shoulder. I wanted to lean into him and steal his strength, but I didn't deserve that. So I just stood there.

"Thank you," I said. He offered me back the note. The

paper felt so flimsy in my hands. My sister's future was about to rip like the paper. I needed all the help I could get. "I need to call some people."

"Of course," he agreed.

"I have an uncle in California," I said, more just to keep myself talking and from freaking out rather than actually trying to communicate. "He might be able to help. At least he's a lot closer."

"Yes," he agreed. He gave my shoulder a gentle squeeze. "I'm so sorry."

"Thank you, Mr. Darcy," I told him.

"Call me William," he replied.

I nodded, unable to speak anymore. Tears were threatening to spill out all over the place.

"I'll leave you now," he said, giving me one last squeeze. "Please call me if you need anything."

I nodded again, pulling out my phone and looking for my uncle's phone number. I wasn't sure if I could get a hold of him at this hour, but I had to try. I wondered what time it was wherever my parents were.

I wondered what my mother was going to say.

The front door shut with a soft shush and click. Mr. Darcy was gone. I suddenly felt less strong than I had a moment ago. I could only imagine what kind of terrible situation Lydia was in. There was nothing good that an out-of-work agent could do with a broke girl. I just hoped I was wrong.

I took a deep breath and dialed the phone, wishing with all my heart that Mr. Darcy still had his hand on my shoulder.

Chapter 19

*T*hirty-some-odd hours later, I was no closer to finding my sister.

"Any word on Lydia?" Jane asked, coming into the kitchen. I sat at the table, searching my phone.

I shook my head. "I called the police, but she's an adult, and she isn't really missing," I told her. "And California is a big place."

"I'm so sorry, Lizzie." Jane put her hands on my shoulders and gave me a reassuring squeeze.

"My uncle is driving down from Sacramento today, but I'm not sure how much help it's going to be," I continued. "I forgot that our Mom and Dad were in the middle of the ocean on their cruise. I can't even get ahold of them. Even so, they couldn't do anything even if I could reach them."

I looked down at my cereal and realized I hadn't eaten a bite of it. It was now just soggy mush.

"How are you doing?" Jane asked. I could tell she was worried about me.

"I didn't sleep the night of the party, and I didn't sleep much last night. I just kept looking up and calling hotels," I told her. I played with the soggy cereal with my spoon. I wasn't hungry anyway. "She's been in California for forty-eight hours, and I haven't had a word from her. I worried."

"I'm sure she's fine," Jane told me, but she didn't sound like she fully believed it herself.

"I booked a ticket for a flight out," I told her. "I was able to get a red-eye. It's the earliest I could get." I sighed and stared at my breakfast mush. "I don't know what I'm going to do there, but I can't just sit and do nothing."

"You'll find her," Jane promised. I wanted to believe her so badly.

"I can't believe she did this," I said. Frustration welled up inside my chest and threatened to consume me. "She has no real money, she doesn't know anyone out there, and she makes stupid decisions if someone tells her it will make her famous. I should have told her about Wickham."

"We couldn't have known this was going to happen," Jane replied. "This isn't your fault."

"I am supposed to look out for her," I replied, my voice coming out harsher than I intended. "She's my little sister."

Jane didn't take my sharp tone personally. "Maybe it's nothing," she told me, looking on the bright side. "Maybe she really does have a real shot at an acting role. Just because he was fired doesn't mean he can't still have connections."

I just looked at her. There was no way in hell that was even remotely possible.

Jane shrugged in acknowledgment of how ridiculous she sounded. "I'm just trying to make you feel better."

I hardly acknowledged her. I just pushed my bowl of mush away.

Jane patted my shoulder and took the bowl to the sink

for me. I stared out the window for a minute as she did my dishes. Jane was good to me.

I chewed my lip. There was something else I needed to ask Jane.

"Hey, I heard that Charles is back in New York," I said after a moment. I turned in my chair to look at her.

Jane froze for a split second before putting on a fake smile. "I heard that too," she replied. She shrugged casually. "But, we don't exactly run in the same social circles, so I don't think that I'll run into him."

She went back to scrubbing my cereal bowl with a vengeance.

"Are you okay?" I asked. I thought about getting up and helping, but the way she was attacking the bowl made me nervous. If I got too close, she might scrub me.

"I'm fine," she replied, her voice flat. "I'm totally over him. He broke my heart, but I'm over it. I've moved on."

I raised my eyebrows as she looked over at me. I didn't believe a word of it.

"If I saw him on the street, I would simply wave and keep going," she informed me, holding the scrub brush in a death grip. "No big deal."

She turned and attacked the already sparkling kitchen sink. Our apartment was so clean she was going to have to start asking neighbors to clean their apartments just to have something dirty to tackle.

"Okay, then," I told her. "If I see him, though, I'm going to punch him."

"Lizzie!" Jane turned nearly threw the scrub brush at me before realizing it was a joke. "Don't do that. Don't punch people."

"Fine. I promise." I grinned at her. "Besides, he's got security guards. I'd never get close enough."

Jane chuckled and shook her head at me. "You did once."

I shared a wry smile back at her. "You're right. I did once."

We shared a laugh. Then she sighed and grabbed the Clorox from under the sink, then began to scrub. I wondered how much a stainless steel sink would cost since she was going to scrub the varnish clean off of ours. It had to be half an inch thinner from just her scrubbing it this month.

I sighed and checked my phone for any messages or updates from Lydia.

There were, of course, none.

I tried to keep the rising panic in my chest under control by checking on the status of my flight tonight. I had no real plans of what I was going to do once I got to California, but I hoped just being in the right city would help my search.

And, if heaven forbid, Lydia needed me to rescue her from a terrible situation, I would be there and not a six-hour flight away.

I was mentally packing my bags with what I would need to bring and what could fit in a carry-on when the apartment door opened.

In walked Lydia with a big smile.

"Lydia?" I stood up, sure I was hallucinating. "Oh, thank god!"

I ran to her, wrapping my arms around her neck and holding her to me. My little sister was home and safe. She was fine.

"What in the world is up with you?" Lydia asked, gently pulling away. She looked at me like I'd lost my mind. She turned and instructed the man behind her. "Just put my bag inside here, Jeeves. Thank you."

I watched as a uniformed man lugged her massive suitcase inside the door. I hurried to grab him a tip which he gratefully accepted before nodding his head and heading back down to his car.

"We were so worried about you," Jane told her, running over to hug Lydia as well. I was glad to see she'd left the scrub brush at the sink.

"Worried about what?" Lydia scoffed. She threw her hair over her shoulder, just like I imagined a Hollywood actress would.

"You went to California," Jane replied. "With Wickham. And you didn't call."

Lydia sighed like we were the ones being dramatic. "I didn't have time to call. I have a real agent now," she told us. "There's no way I don't become a star now."

"A real agent?" Jane repeated. "I don't understand. What happened with Wickham?"

"He's old news," she said, waving her hand through the air like we should have already known.

I stared at her, my mouth open. Jane quickly came over and took Lydia's elbow before I smacked her.

"How about you come sit down and tell us what happened?" Jane asked, smiling and pulling her toward the table. "I'm afraid we aren't well-versed in Hollywood."

"Oh, I wouldn't expect you to be, Jane," Lydia replied. She smiled and sat at the head of the kitchen table. I stood off to the side with my arms crossed near the window.

I looked out the window just in time to see a limo drive away from our building. It had the Oceanic Airlines' logo painted on the roof. More questions swirled in my head as Lydia cleared her throat.

"So, I told Wickham that I wasn't an heiress," she began. "You would have been proud of me, Lizzie. He didn't care, but he did tell me that he had just gotten a new idea for me."

"Right after you told him you weren't rich?" I clarified.

"Yeah, but the timing was just coincidence. It had nothing to do with the deal he was about to set up for me."

I managed to keep from rolling my eyes, and let her continue.

"Anyway, he brought me out to Los Angeles," she continued. "I was supposed to meet with this big producer tonight in his hotel room."

"Wait a second," I interjected, unable to contain myself any more. "You were meeting with a producer in his hotel room? At night?"

Lydia rolled her eyes. "Yes. It's very normal, okay?" She looked at me like I was the crazy one.

"If you say so," Jane said, pacifying the situation. "Please continue, Lydia."

"*Anyway*, it was about lunchtime yesterday when Wickham went off to set up some more meetings for me. He said he had other producers that were interested in my talents," Lydia continued.

"I'm sure they were," I muttered under my breath. Lydia didn't hear me, but Jane glared at me.

"I went for a walk out in the California sunshine. I have to say that my hair and makeup were on point," Lydia continued. "I looked good. So, I was just standing by the side of the road, minding my own business, when this limo pulls up. The window opened, and no joke, it's Abram Jones."

"Who's Abram Jones?" I asked. Lydia rolled her eyes and glared at me.

"Who's Abram Jones?" Jane repeated in a much gentler tone. Lydia patted her hand and smiled.

"He's just the biggest agent in Hollywood," she told Jane

with a small chuckle. "He has all the major stars signed to him. Actors wait years just to be introduced to him, and he pulled up and asked to be introduced to me."

She giggled and looked around the table. Apparently, we were supposed to be in awe.

"Oh, wow," I replied. Lydia sighed, obviously unimpressed with my lack of excitement.

Jane's phone buzzed. "Shoot, excuse me for a second. Keep going, Lydia. I just have to take this call. It's work."

Jane got up and went to the living room. I could hear her talking to someone on the other line.

Lydia didn't wait to continue her story. "So, I got in the limo, and-"

"Wait, you just got in a limo with a strange man?" I interrupted. "What were you thinking?"

"You do it every time you get in a cab, Lizzie," Lydia snapped back at me. "Besides, Mr. Darcy was with him, so I knew it was okay."

His name hit me like a bag of bricks.

"Mr. Darcy was with him?" I asked, taking a step forward.

"Shoot. I wasn't supposed to tell you that," Lydia said. She pouted. "Please forget I said anything about him."

I blinked twice. How was I supposed to forget something like that? Lydia just sat there, waiting for me to promise. She wasn't going to continue her story until I said something.

"Okay, what'd I miss?" Jane asked, returning to the table. Lydia looked at me, her arms crossed.

"Lydia got in a limo with a strange man she didn't know," I replied. "No one else was in there. Go on, Lydia."

"Good." Lydia smiled and adjusted her shoulders to sit taller. "I got in, and he says that he loves my head-shots and that he has the perfect role for me. The part is basically mine. It's a smaller film, and it's only a supporting role, but Oprah Winfrey won a Best Supporting Actress Oscar for her debut role, so I think it'll be fine. Besides, I think starting in a smaller role really adds to the allure of coming from nothing and making it big."

I just stared at my sister. I didn't even know where to begin with that. How in the world were we related? There had to have been a genetic mix-up somewhere.

"What happened with Wickham?" Jane asked, bringing the conversation back to where we started.

"Oh, right." Lydia took a breath. "Since I had met with Abram, oh- he asked me to call him Abram, I didn't need to meet with the producer that night. In fact, Abram told me not to. He had me get on a plane and come home right away so I can start preparing for my role."

If nothing else, I liked this Abram. He got my sister to come home.

"I got to fly home on a private jet," Lydia continued. "It was Abram's. By coincidence, he happened to have bought it from your friend Mr. Darcy last year. It felt so luxurious and right to be on there. I don't think I can ever fly normally again."

"How nice," I replied. There was more to this story than Lydia was telling me and most of it revolved around Mr. Darcy. What in the world had he done to bring my sister home? I could only imagine what hiring an agent like Abram must have cost.

I sat down hard on one of the kitchen chairs and looked over at my sister. She had no idea what Mr. Darcy had done for her.

"What are you looking at me like that for?" Lydia crossed her arms.

"Do you have any idea how lucky you were?" I asked her.

I thought of all the bad things that had gone through my mind and shuddered.

"Well, yeah." Lydia grinned innocently. "I just got my big break."

I just sighed. She had no clue how close she'd come to losing that innocence.

"And don't worry, Lizzie, you're invited to all my premiers." She smiled at me. "You and Jane are family. You two are going to get the perks of my fame. Like free sunglasses."

I couldn't help but shake my head and smile. Somehow, she managed to make me not want to murder her again with the simple promise of sunglasses.

"I'm going to go freshen up and then head to the gym," Lydia announced. "I have to look good for next week."

She grinned at Jane and me, and then bounced off to her room. Her long brown ponytail swung happily from side to side as she went. I just stared at her, glad she was still the same old Lydia. It was so much better than the alternative.

"Well, that wasn't what I was expecting," Jane commented as Lydia closed her bedroom door.

"Yup," I agreed.

"How did she manage that? There's no way that was a random event," Jane said. She shook her head and sat back in her chair.

"I think Mr. Darcy might have had something to do with it," I said after a moment. Guilt pulled at me.

"No, no way," Jane replied. "Not after what he's done to you."

"I may have been wrong about him." I shifted uncomfortably in my chair. "I actually don't think he's quite as much of a jerk as I first thought."

Jane raised her eyebrows and looked sternly at me. "You were wrong?"

"Maybe." I shrugged uncomfortably. I hated admitting I was wrong.

Jane nodded once. "Right." She looked over at Lydia's door and then back to me. "And on that strange note, I'm going to go to work now. Have fun with Lydia and trying to get her to accept any form of responsibility."

I snorted. "Right. Because that's gonna happen this century."

"Have fun," Jane told me, standing up and grabbing her bag by the front door. She waved one last time before heading out.

I sat in the now empty kitchen letting relief wash over me. My little sister was safe and was now in a much better position. She wasn't going to get scammed and tricked by trying to follow her dreams. It meant I didn't have to be afraid for her.

And there was only one person that could have made that happen.

I had to see him.

Chapter 20

I stared up at the tall building just outside of Central Park that Mr. Darcy worked at. I'd verified that it was the right one on the walk over and I even knew which office was his. I hoped that I could see him and thank him for what he'd just done for my family. I just had to get past security and his secretaries.

The lobby was full of windows and bright, modern architecture. There were two sets of elevators, but to get to them, I had to get past security. I squared my shoulders and walked up.

"Hello, I'm here to see Mr. Darcy," I announced. My voice squeaked a little.

"Name?" The big guard asked.

"Elizabeth Bennet," I replied. "I just need to see him for a minute. I'm sure if you tell him I'm here he'll let me come up, and I just really need to see him."

The security guard waited until I stopped babbling. "Ma'am, you're already on the approved list. Take the second elevator to the top. Have a nice day."

"Oh."

I nodded and walked past him to the elevator and got on. Mr. Darcy had me on his list. There was no way that he could have known that I would ever come here, but yet I was allowed to. He wanted me to.

I love you...

The memory of him telling me that in the rain came back like a whisper. My cheeks flushed, and guilt pulled at my stomach. I was a fool.

The top floor matched the lobby. It was all clean lines and modern furniture in the blue and white of Oceania Airlines. A painter stood off in one of the corners slowly adding green accents.

"Excuse me," I said, walking up to a large desk with a woman wearing a headset. "I'd like to see Mr. Darcy. I'm Elizabeth Bennet."

The woman looked up. "Of course," she said with a smile as she checked her schedule and list of approved contacts. Her eyes widened slightly before she looked at me again. "Please have a seat. He's finishing a meeting, but once he's done, you may see him."

"Thank you," I told her.

I found a seat in the white lobby and looked out the window. I could see Central Park from here. The leaves were gone from the trees leaving stark gray lines across the gray grass. The sky sparkled with wispy white clouds across the sea of blue. The color of the sky reminded me of Mr. Darcy's eyes when he smiled.

"Ms. Bennet?" The secretary stood next to me. "Mr. Darcy will see you now."

"Oh, thank you," I replied. I had been so lost in the blue sky that I didn't see her leave her desk. She brought me to a glass door and held it open as I walked in.

The office was dominated by a large, sleek, modern desk.

The view was even better in here. I could see more of the city and all of the park below. On either side of the window, books lined the walls in all shapes and sizes.

Everything was very elegant and smooth. I suddenly felt very out of place in my jeans and t-shirt. I was just glad that my black wool jacket was nice. It was my saving feature.

"Elizabeth," Mr. Darcy greeted me as I stepped in. He stood and came to the front of his desk. He wore his traditional perfectly fitted suit. Today was a beautiful dark blue that brought out the darkness of his hair and the light blues of his eyes. "What can I do for you?"

All the grand speeches I practiced on the way over went right out the window. I'd had this beautiful thank you speech all planned out, and now that I was here, standing in front of him, I couldn't remember a word of it.

"I, um, I..." I stopped and took a deep breath. There was no reason to be nervous, yet my stomach was dancing with butterflies. "I wanted to thank you."

"For what?" he said like he didn't know.

"For helping my sister," I replied. I took a step closer to his desk.

"I'm afraid I don't know what you're talking about," he told me with a small shrug. I would have believed him if I didn't know better.

"She let it slip that you were there," I informed him.

He sighed. "Of course she did."

"It wasn't hard to put the pieces together of what you did for her." I took another step into his domain. "There's no other reason for an agent like that to be interested in her."

"I happened to have business in California," he replied. "It was just luck."

I took another step. I was now only a few feet away from him.

"Still, thank you," I told him. I looked up at his face, watching the way his eyes focused on me. It did strange things to my heart. "It means the world to me."

"You love her," he said softly, his eyes still taking me in. "Despite her flaws, you love her."

He opened his mouth as if he were going to say more, but instead took a breath and turned from me. I missed his gaze as soon as it was gone. It made the room less bright.

There was silence in the room.

"I should have brought you a fruit basket or something," I said with a laugh, wanting to make him smile. "I think I need to work on my thank yous."

He chuckled softly. "My secretary would have just stolen it."

I smiled, liking that he was looking at me again. Those blue eyes held more in them than the sky outside.

A knock came on the door behind me. "Sir, your ten o'clock is here," his secretary said, opening the door and peeking her head in for a moment.

"Thank you," he told her, but his eyes didn't leave me. He looked at me like I was beautiful, even in my jeans and coat.

"I should go. You have a meeting," I said, not wanting to leave but not wanting to be a bother either. "Thank you. Again."

"Oh, um. One more thing before you go," he said, turning around to his bookshelf. "This came today, from the hospital. I wouldn't even know what to do with it, but I have a feeling that you do."

He handed me a box wrapped in cellophane. I recognized the box as the one from the auction. The one that contained the 18th century journal that I had bid on for my father.

I looked up at him, and he looked down at me. I had no idea what to say to express how I felt.

I told my feet to move, but they didn't want to leave Mr. Darcy. I couldn't blame them. Instead of turning to the door, I took the last step to him and went up on tiptoe to kiss him on the cheek. It was chaste compared to our other kisses, but still, the electricity of it made my heart skip.

"I hope your meeting goes well," I said, taking a step back and nearly running into who I assumed was his ten o'clock. "Oh, excuse me."

The woman I'd nearly knocked over didn't give me the time of day. She wore a smart pantsuit and her dark gray hair was short and severe. She was somewhat scary, even though she barely came up to my shoulder. She was not someone to be trifled with.

I quickly ran out the door, my lips still hot with the kiss. I looked back to see him smile at me before greeting the woman.

"Hello, Catherine," he said, and the rest was lost as the door closed.

I held my hand to my lips, my heart pounding. Why had I kissed him? Why had I come here? He didn't want to be thanked. He had done this without telling me, yet here I was. I was a glutton for punishment, I decided. I liked the way Mr. Darcy put me off balance.

I nodded to the secretary and escaped down the elevators and out to the lobby. My lips still tingled, and I couldn't wipe the smile off my face. I felt lighter than I had in months and I knew it had to do with Mr. Darcy.

I needed to see Jane. I needed to tell her that I'd seen him.

Outside his building, the wind was cold and sharp. It felt good against my hot cheeks, and I loosened the buttons on my jacket. Everything was hot from being with him. I stepped out onto the sidewalk and looked up toward his office. It was silly, but I thought I could see him looking down at me.

I waved and smiled, even though it was stupid. It probably wasn't even his office, yet I liked the idea of him watching me and smiling.

Chapter 21

I knew the way to the art museum with my eyes closed. I loved visiting Jane at her work. The museum was always full of beautiful objects, but the backroom where she worked at restoring priceless artwork was the true treasure trove.

I waved to the security guard and docent who smiled and waved back as I headed to the work area. I slipped through a work door and followed the scent of paint. Jane was at a speckled sink cleaning her brushes.

"Guess who?" I said, stepping out from behind a canvas.

Jane grinned. "Lizzie! What a nice surprise. I was just about to stop for lunch. Want to join me?"

I nodded and came around to stand by the sink as she methodically worked the brushes clean.

"I'd love to," I told her. "I need a drink."

She glanced over at me. "What happened in the last two hours that requires a drink?" Concern flickered across her face. "It's not Lydia, is it?"

"No, no. Lydia's fine," I told her. I took a deep breath and stood before her. "I think I like him."

Jane just frowned. "Like who?"

I hesitated, but Jane was my best friend. If I couldn't tell her, then I wouldn't be able to tell anyone.

"Mr. Darcy."

Jane laughed. "Are you serious?" She laughed some more before looking at my face and seeing that I was. "Oh. My."

"Yeah."

She managed to look thoughtful for about two seconds before cracking up. "You can't be serious, Lizzie," she said, trying to keep herself composed. "Do I need to send you the video of the two of you arguing? You hate him. You slapped him in the face the first time you met him. You don't like him."

"I didn't say he wasn't an ass," I retorted, crossing my arms. I didn't like her laughing at me. "I said I might love him."

That sobered her up fast. "Whoa."

"I mean, like. I meant I *like* him." I tried to cover it up, but it was too late. I'd said the L word.

"Oh, nononono," Jane replied. She wasn't laughing anymore. "You don't make a slip like that without meaning it."

I slumped against the wall. "Then you get my problem."

"Oh, Lizzie." Jane sighed and put her brushes away to dry. She picked up a towel and dried her hands. "What are we going to do with you?"

"Buy me a drink?" I offered. "That's a good thing to do with me."

Jane chuckled and put her arm around my shoulder. "All right. Come with me."

Together we walked out of the back area and into the main museum. I loved this place nearly as much as Jane did.

There were big windows down the main corridor that let in lots of natural light but kept the paintings out of the sun. Beautiful works of art filled the space, creating a tranquil sea of emotions captured forever.

Jane stopped short, nearly knocking me over in the process. She stood rock still in the middle of the gallery staring straight ahead and going pale. One look at her face told me what she saw, and sure enough, there he was.

Standing in the center of the sunlit gallery was Charles Bingley.

His reddish hair was neatly combed back, and he wore a suit that reminded me of Mr. Darcy's. He stood strong, but I could see his hands shaking even from this distance. He was staring hard at Jane.

"Jane?" he called out her name. His voice didn't shake, though.

Jane was as much a statue as any sculpture in the room. I gave her a gentle push on the shoulder to make her take a step forward. She glanced at me, fear in her eyes. I motioned her toward him

"At least hear what he has to say," I whispered.

She nodded and took a hesitant couple of steps, stopping short of being near him.

"Hello, Charles," she whispered. I sent as much positive energy her direction as I could.

"Jane, I came to apologize," Charles announced. He took a step toward her and then hesitated.

"For what?" Jane asked, her voice coming in slightly stronger.

Charles took a deep breath. He looked around the room and then focused on her. His eyes softened, and he smiled. He took another step.

"I'm sorry for ever leaving you," he told her. He went to

one knee and held up a small, black velvet box. Everyone, even me, gasped. "Never leave me again."

He opened the box and presented it to her. Even from where I was standing, I could see the glimmer of a diamond.

Jane stood there for a moment, then slowly nodded. A combination of a sob and a laugh left her as she flung herself down and into Charles' arms.

"Yes," she whispered, still laughing and crying at the same time.

I pulled out my phone and quickly snapped a picture, knowing that Jane would want the memory. It was beautiful. He had her in his arms as they were surrounded by the beautiful works of art they both so loved.

He'd picked the perfect place to propose. This was Jane's pride and joy. Proposing here demonstrated that he did know her. He loved her. The whole room radiated with their love, and it was more beautiful than the art.

I wiped a tear from my cheek and smiled. I was so incredibly happy for Jane. Something bittersweet tugged on my heart. Mr. Darcy was behind this, too. I knew it. He had told his friend to go back to Jane. He'd admitted he was wrong.

Charles was helping Jane stand. She just held onto him and smiled wider than I'd ever seen her smile before. She radiated such joy, and she wasn't going to let him go anytime soon.

I looked around, watching the art patrons clap and cheer. A dark figure by the door caught my attention. It was Mr. Darcy. He smiled as he caught my eye before turning and disappearing out into the street.

I went to catch him, to thank him yet again for making the people I cared most about happy, but Jane called my name. I turned to answer, and I knew he was gone. I looked one last time and then headed over to congratulate Jane and Charles on their soon to be happily ever after.

Chapter 22

A few days later, I sat behind the nurses' station filling out paperwork. Despite going to a paperless system years ago, I still somehow managed to have mountains of paperwork for my patients. I just wanted to finish and head home. I'd already reported to the night nurses, so once I finished putting in the last few sets of vitals and notes, I could leave.

A shower and bed sounded like the best thing in the world.

"Hey, Lizzie," the charge nurse called to me. "There's someone here to see you."

Lydia and Jane rarely visited me at work, and if they did, it was always at lunchtime so I could buy them cafeteria food. I knew it wasn't them, and despite my dreams, I knew that Mr. Darcy would never show up here.

I sighed, hit save, closed my screens, and went to see who wanted me. Maybe it was a former patient. Those always made my day.

It was not a patient.

I came to the entrance of the unit to find a woman in an

expensive pantsuit and a mean look on her face waiting for me. She looked like a grandmother, but without any of the requisite kindness. I recognized her from Mr. Darcy's office.

I had a bad feeling about this. I just wanted to go home and take a shower.

"Do you know who I am?" the woman barked as soon as I got near. She had the same accent as Mr. Darcy, except his sounded much suaver. Her's sounded mean.

"You're Catherine de Bourgh, Mr. Darcy's COO," I replied politely. Maybe she had a legit reason to be here. I hoped that Mr. Darcy was okay.

"Good. You're not as stupid as you look," the woman replied.

I bit my tongue. "How can I help you, Ms. de Bourgh?"

"Can we speak privately?" She gestured toward the gaggle of nurses trying to overhear what was going on.

"Of course. There's a doctor consult room over here," I told her, motioning down the hallway. We stepped into a small room with four comfortable chairs and a table. A whiteboard hung on the wall opposite of the door.

"I'm sure you know why I'm here," Catherine announced as soon as she stepped into the room. Her small statue somehow dominated the entire thing.

"I'm afraid I don't," I said, shaking my head. "Is Mr. Darcy alright?"

"That's what I'm here to see to." She looked around the room in disapproval before coming back to me. She somehow looked less pleased as she looked me over. "Why were you in Mr. Darcy's office yesterday?"

"I wanted to thank him," I replied honestly. "He did something kind for me."

"No other reason?" she pressed. "You did kiss him."

"I did," I confirmed. She walked around the small room

as I spoke, making me feel like I was being interrogated by a caged tiger. "I kissed him in gratitude because, as I said, he did something kind for me. He is a good man."

Catherine spun on her heel, surprising me with a sudden advance into my personal space. "Do you intend to seduce my nephew?" she asked, point blank. "Because I will not allow that."

"Excuse me?" I asked, completely taken aback.

"He is needed by this company," Catherine informed me, not really explaining herself. "He is the life force of this company, and you cannot distract him." Her eyes narrowed. "Have you been sent by a competitor?"

"What? Ma'am, I have no idea what you are talking about," I replied, taking a step back. She continued to stay in my face.

"He left a very important meeting to go to California for no reason," Catherine told me. She kept stepping forward, making me retreat. "The buyout nearly failed because of it, and I want to know why. I flew all the way from London. You're the only reason I can come up with."

"Ma'am, I'm afraid I don't have any explanation for you," I stated, using my best customer service voice. I didn't add on, *"and even if I did, there's no way in hell I'd tell you,"* because that seemed like a worse idea than taunting a bear.

"I will not allow you to destroy everything I have worked so hard to achieve," the small woman shrieked at me. Her tone set my teeth on edge.

"You mean what Mr. Darcy has worked so hard to achieve," I corrected her. I was fine with her talking down to me, but not him. It was his company. Not hers.

"You are impertinent!" She took a step back, mouth open and unhappy. "You will leave William alone. You are not his equal. You are nothing but a harlot out for his money."

My mouth opened in shock. She was furious, and I could do nothing but stand there and take it. "Ma'am-"

"I saw you in his office yesterday. I saw the way he looked at you," she sneered. "I know what your sister is willing to do for fame. Your whole family stinks of scandal. I know it all, and I will not tolerate it!"

I couldn't believe she was speaking to me this way. All I wanted was my shower. I took a deep breath, drawing on reserves of calm I didn't know I had.

"Ma'am, thank you for taking the time out of your very busy schedule to make sure that I know my place," I told her, doing my best to keep my temper in line. "Now, please excuse me. I have work to do."

I pushed past her to get to the exit, but she slammed her hand down on the table hard enough to make me jump.

"You selfish girl!" she snarled. "Do you think that I do this for him? I do this for the company. How dare you put his company at risk for your greed and lust!"

I bit my tongue hard enough to draw blood.

"I'm afraid I don't understand what you think I'm doing," I told her. "I am hardly a distraction."

Catherine narrowed her eyes. "Don't play coy, young lady. It doesn't become you," she sneered. "William's place is in London with his company. Not here in New York. This is a temporary stop, and I will not have him move his headquarters here. I will not let him throw away the company we have built."

"He's moving his headquarters?" I asked, surprised. "Why?"

"He says New York is the better location," Catherine spat. "I say it's you. You have tainted his mind and made him, and now me, come to this wretched city."

"I didn't make you, or Mr. Darcy do anything," I told her. "Least of all have him move his headquarters."

"Now, swear to me that you will leave him. Swear to me that you will leave him to his work, and tell him to go back to London," the old woman pressed. She came forward and stuck her finger under my nose. "You are beneath him, and I will not have him throw it all away for a stupid girl who only wants his cash flow."

I was so angry I was unaccountably calm. Maybe it was because I was at work. Maybe it was because I was tired. Maybe the stars had simply aligned, but for once, I was furious yet able to keep my wits about me.

"I will not."

She glared at me and reached for her purse. "Fine. How much will it take?" She pulled out a checkbook.

"Excuse me?" I asked, not quite following.

"How much money to leave him alone?" she asked. She looked me over once. "You look like fifty thousand would make your life better."

"No." I didn't even hesitate.

"Fine." She scribbled numbers on the check and ripped it out, holding it up to me. "One hundred thousand dollars never to see him again."

The idea that she thought she could buy me was infuriating.

"There is no amount of money you can offer me," I informed her, still floating in my calm anger. "I will see him as he sees fit. If he wishes to see me, then he may. It is his decision, not yours."

"I do what is best for him!" Catherine shrieked at me. She was not calm. She did not have my cool, detached anger right now.

"No, I care for him. I respect him," I told her. "You are

doing neither of those things by showing up here and trying to buy me off. Now, you will leave, or I will have security escort you out."

Despite my calm bubble, I was shaking with rage. I had never wanted to beat the crap out of someone so badly, yet I managed to keep myself standing with my hands to myself.

"You intolerable whore!" Catherine screamed at me. I was glad these doctor consult rooms were soundproofed. I opened the door leading out to the hallway and held it open for her.

"You have now insulted me in every possible way," I informed her, surprised at the even control in my voice. I felt like screaming, but I wasn't. I spoke evenly and calmly. "You can have nothing further left to discuss. Good night, Ma'am. If I see you again, I will call security."

"How dare you!" Catherine screamed at me. She sounded like a bitter, broken old woman. If I hadn't been so furious, I would have pitied her.

She stepped out into the hallway and stomped away. Her heels clicked on the floor hard enough to drive holes into the linoleum, but I just stood there, making sure she left my unit.

"Are you okay out there, Lizzie?" one of the nurse's asked, peeking her head into the hallway. Maybe the doctor consult rooms weren't quite as soundproofed as I thought.

"It's fine," I told my coworker as I headed back to my computer. I still had to finish my work. "It was just an angry old woman."

I went to an empty patient room and shut the door so that I could finish charting in peace. I was still shaking and furious, yet oddly calm. I didn't quite understand it.

I couldn't believe that Catherine had come to my hospital. I replayed the entire visit in my head, trying to make it make sense. I wasn't a threat to Mr. Darcy's business. He would have to want to be in New York all the time to make his headquarters here. He loved London. Why would he do that?

For me?

That was laughable, and yet...

It made hope flare up for a moment before I put it back in its place.

I had burned the bridge between the two of us. I could cry at the ashes all I wanted, but I was the one that lit the match. As much as I wished this conversation and him moving his headquarters meant something, I knew he wasn't mine and never would be.

Chapter 23

*T*wo days later I woke before dawn. It was my day off, so I didn't need to be awake, yet I couldn't go back to sleep. I itched to get up and move. My brain was too full and my heart too tender to sit in bed and think.

I put on my favorite black exercise pants and a soft sweatshirt. Outside, the dark air frosted with every breath and ice hung on the tree branches and buildings as I walked to Central Park. It was quiet in the early gray morning. There were only a few runners pounding the pavement, but they kept to themselves, huffing and puffing like dragons in the gray light.

It was as close to being alone in the city as I could get.

A layer of snow glistened and glimmered on the grass. No one had disturbed it yet, so it was still perfect and white. For a moment, I could imagine that there were no other people in the entire world. It was just me and the cold.

I wished the cold could freeze my hope. I wished that it could freeze the ache inside of me every time I thought about him. I couldn't stop thinking about him and how much I cared for him. It was terrible torture to know he was in the same city and yet not knowing how to tell him what was in my heart.

The icy ground crackled under my feet with every step. The sky glowed red with the upcoming day, but the sun hadn't yet risen. I took a deep breath, feeling the cold enter me. I held the freezing air inside of me, focusing on it until it warmed.

That's when I saw him.

Mr. Darcy walked along the path. He wore a long, black pea coat that made him look like a hero from the past. It suited him. He walked like he was trying to clear his mind just like I was. Long, steady steps but with no clear destination.

He looked up and saw me. He paused and his breath frosted the air. My heart sped up as he kept walking toward me instead of turning away.

"What are you doing out here?" he asked me, looking at the frozen landscape and my light jacket. "You must be freezing."

"I couldn't sleep," I told him. I wondered if he could hear the thrill in my voice at finding him this morning.

"Nor I," he replied. His lips thinned. "Did my COO speak to you?"

I gave a slow nod. "Yes, she did." I wasn't quite sure how much more detail I wanted to go into. Just thinking of her telling me to stay away from him made my blood boil.

"I'm sorry," he apologized. "She shouldn't have done that. I've spoken to her about it and sent her back to London. What can I do to fix it?"

"Fix it?" I repeated. I shook my head. "After what you did for Lydia, and for Jane, I should be thanking you and seeing if you need anything fixed."

I smiled up at him and was caught in those blue eyes. They held me and warmed me just by looking at me.

"You must know," he said softly. "You must know it was for you. It was always for you."

He smiled so sadly that I was afraid my heart might break.

I reached out and took his hand. He had no gloves, and his fingers were like ice.

"Did you mean what you said to Catherine?" he asked, his face cautious and words quiet.

"Yes," I replied. I wrapped my fingers around him, sending him my warmth. "I meant every word to her."

"So I can see you whenever I want?" he asked. I looked up at his face and smiled.

"Yes."

"And that you care for me?"

My chest tightened and threatened to explode. If I were to run and protect myself from heartache, this was where I should do it. But that was the last thing I wanted to do.

"Very much," I whispered.

He held his hands perfectly still in mine. All I could think about was how good it felt to touch him. To have this connection with him. I looked up, seeing hope and a small amount of fear cross his face.

"My feelings for you haven't changed. If you tell me to, I will leave you alone forever," he told me, his voice low. He swallowed hard and looked me in the eye. "But, if your feelings have changed, I have to tell you that I'm yours. Body and soul."

He turned his hand to mine, holding my fingers like I might burn him for a second time but that he was willing to risk it. He was willing to risk everything for me once more.

"I love you, Elizabeth," he whispered. His blue eyes shone with the truth of it. "I never stopped."

Time froze as the sun came over the horizon and lit the world in brilliant glory. The snow sparkled like a million tiny diamonds, each reflecting my heart's desire back at me.

"I love you, too, Mr. Darcy," I whispered back. My mouth said the words with ease because my heart was singing them.

"Call me William," he replied with a widening smile. And then he kissed me.

Chapter 24

One Year Later
New Years Eve

LONDON STOOD out before me in all its glory. Every building was lit up in preparation for the new year. In just five minutes, this year, the most beautiful year of my life would end, and the next would begin.

For the first time in a long time, I was excited and sad for the new year. I would miss this year only because it had been so wonderful, but my excitement over what was coming next made it more than bearable. With William at my side, my world would always be better each and every year.

"Come get your champagne for the toast," Jane called to me from the kitchen. Standing with her fiancee, she had never looked more beautiful or radiant. In just two months, she would make the most beautiful bride I'd ever seen. I couldn't wait for their year-long engagement to be over.

"Don't spill it all over my brother's kitchen," Georgiana chided, coming up behind her with a dishcloth. Since the doctors had declared her in remission several months ago, her face had filled out, though she still kept her hair in that pixie cut.

She shook her head. "You Americans have no idea how to pour champagne."

Charles laughed and added more champagne to Georgiana's glass. She grinned at him. "That's better."

"I'll get yours, Elizabeth," Mr. Darcy told me. He grinned before heading into the kitchen and Georgiana chuckled as she handed him a glass.

My phone buzzed in my pocket. Only three minutes to go.

I pulled out my cellphone out to find a message from Lydia. She was safely in California and on the set for her new movie. She sent me a selfie of her outside with the cast and crew as they prepped to start filming the follow-up to her debut film.

I texted her back that she looked great and to break a leg. I'd see her for the Oscar's Award Ceremony in just a few months. We were going to rock the red carpet together this year.

She was favored to win the Oscar for Best Supporting Actress for her debut role.

"Are you ready, my love?" William asked me coming up and wrapping his arms around my waist.

I sighed with contentment and leaned into him as we looked out at the city together.

"I am, Mr. Darcy," I told him. He chuckled and shook his head.

"You just love calling me that, don't you?"

I grinned. "I only call you that because I love you. I fell in love with Mr. Darcy."

"And what about poor William?" he asked, spinning me to face him. I loved the way his eyes lit up as he found my face.

"I love him, too," I replied. "But, Mr. Darcy is who you are to me. And I love him with everything I have."

He grinned as the grandfather clock in the library started to chime. It was midnight and the new year had begun. The sound of fireworks filled the air.

Mr. Darcy and I tapped our glasses together and took a sip. The bubbles tickled my nose.

"Look inside," he whispered, his voice cracking. I frowned, looking up at him.

"What?"

"Look inside your champagne," he repeated. I knew that look. It was the same one he wore that day in the park almost a year ago when he told me for the second time that he loved me.

I looked down at my glass. There was far more than just champagne in the flute. There was a ring.

I gasped and looked up at him to find him going to one knee before me.

"Elizabeth Bennet, will you do me the honor of making me the happiest man in the world?" he asked. His voice shook slightly, and I loved him all the more for it. "Marry me?"

I nodded, unable to find the words.

"Say 'yes,' or he'll just keep kneeling," Georgiana shouted. I looked up to see Mr. Darcy's sister, his best friend Charles, and my best friend Jane, all grinning at me. They had all known.

"Yes," I managed to squeak out. I was too happy to speak. I just kept nodding. "Yes, yes, yes!"

Mr. Darcy beamed a smile at me as he fished the ring out of the champagne and put it on my finger. I loved how happy he looked. I loved that smile, and I loved that light in his eyes. It was better than the fireworks outside.

The ring was lovely. A diamond bigger than anything I'd ever seen shimmered up at me from my hand.

"And, I have a smaller one for when you're working and need to wear gloves," Mr. Darcy whispered to me. "Because I know that's important to you."

He took my glass and set it to the side for our new years kiss. The others started to sing Auld Lang Syne in the background, but my world was solely focused on Mr. Darcy, my soon-to-be husband.

He took my chin between his first two fingers and his thumb, tipping my face up to look at him. Then, he gave me a rare smile that made my heart flutter and my knees go weak, even after a year of being together. It still made me tremble that he would smile that way at me.

Our lips came together, love and desire mixing in equal parts. It's passionate and primal, yet so deep that my soul sang with his in harmony.

I brought in the New Year, and the rest of my life, with Mr. Darcy's Kiss.

IF YOU LIKED THIS STORY

*Y*ou might also like:
Saltwater Kisses: A Billionaire Love Story
When small-town girl Emma LaRue won a vacation to an exclusive tropical island, a last minute cancellation meant she would be going by herself. Shy and studious, she never had time to fall in love, and often wondered if she was just meant to be alone. However, that all changed when a handsome stranger literally walked into her life while on the beach and sparks began to fly.

New York's most eligible billionaire bachelor Jack Saunders thought this vacation would be the perfect escape, one last hurrah, before taking full control of his father's company. When an innocent Emma didn't recognize him, he figured that he might get a chance to have a vacation from being rich. He didn't tell her about the cars, the yacht, or the penthouse. All he did was let her fall in love with him.

Soon, Jack found that he was the one falling in love with Emma. When they enjoy a fantasy marriage ceremony on the beach, they thought it was a bit of harmless fun before returning to their normal lives. A bittersweet goodbye was supposed to be the end of their perfect vacation romance, but when photos of the ceremony were leaked to the press, everything changed.

Feeling lied to and thrust into a world of wealth and privilege, Emma must choose between following her dreams or following her heart. Will she be content at being nothing more than the billionaire's wife, or will she return to her normal life with only memories of saltwater kisses?

HE PUSHED me back until I bumped against the door. His mouth skimmed my jaw, down to my throat, his teeth grazing my skin and his five-o-clock shadow scratching gently. He pressed a thigh between my legs, sending heat through my belly and then south. I whimpered for more, the noise low in my throat.

"You want to invite me in?" he whispered in my ear. Goosebumps ran down my arms, but not from cold.

"Why? Are you a vampire?" I asked with a wry smile.

He didn't answer but instead kissed me again, drawing me to him like a magnet. He wrapped his arms around me and pulled on my waist, guiding me through the open door. He released me and I felt woozy on my feet from his kisses. The door thudded softly shut and I licked my lips.

He was perfect in the moonlight. His shoulders were broad, tapering into a tight waist and an ass that my fingers itched to squeeze. The darkness and the wine made me bold, my desire growing by the minute. His eyes caught mine and he smiled, knowing that I was checking him out. Those eyes turned up the flame growing in my belly, now spreading north and south, filling my core with need. The sexual tension wrapped around us like taut guitar strings, filling the room with vibrating desire.

His hands grabbed my hips again, pulling me into him with strong fingers. I wrapped my arms around his shoulders, tangling my fingers in his hair as we stumbled towards the bedroom. A part of me told me that I should stop, that I should think this through, but the other voices in my head quickly drowned her out; I wanted him more than I wanted to breathe...

Saltwater Kisses: A Billionaire Love Story

ABOUT THE AUTHOR

New York Times and USA Today Bestseller Krista Lakes is a thirtysomething who recently rediscovered her passion for writing. She is living happily ever after with her Prince Charming. Her first kid just started preschool and she is happy to welcome her second child into her life, continuing her "Happily Ever After"!

Thank you for supporting an indie author. Anything you can do, whether it be writing a review, or even simply telling a fellow reader that you enjoyed this, helps me out immensely. Thanks!

Krista would love to hear from you! Please contact her at Krista.Lakes@gmail.com or friend her on Facebook!

Further reading:

Kinds of Love
>A Forever Kind of Love
>A Wonderful Kind of Love
>An Endless Kind of Love
>A Hopeful Kind of Love (novella)

Billionaires and Brides

Yours Completely: A Cinderella Love Story
Yours Truly: A Cinderella Love Story
Yours Royally: A Cinderella Love Story

The "Kisses" series

Saltwater Kisses: A Billionaire Love Story
Kisses From Jack: The Other Side of Saltwater Kisses
Rainwater Kisses: A Billionaire Love Story
Champagne Kisses: A Timeless Love Story
Freshwater Kisses: A Billionaire Love Story
Sandcastle Kisses: A Billionaire Love Story
Hurricane Kisses: A Billionaire Love Story
Barefoot Kisses: A Billionaire Love Story
Sunrise Kisses: A Billionaire Love Story
Waterfall Kisses: A Billionaire Love Story
Island Kisses: A Billionaire Love Story

Other Novels

I Choose You: A Secret Billionaire Romance
Burned: A New Adult Love Story
Walking on Sunshine: A Sweet Summer Romance